HOLLOW MAN

By Todd Sullivan

MOCHA MEMØIRS PRESS

Rock Hill, SC

COPYRIGHT NOTICE

ISBN: 978-0-9998522-7-9

Cover Art by

Editor: Nicole Givens Kurtz

Proofreader: Noella Handley

Publisher: Mocha Memoirs Press

OTHER MOCHA MEMOIRS FANTASY TITLES

Other Mocha Memoirs Fantasy titles

Mutiny on the Moonbeam by Rie Sheridan Rose

The Soul Cages by Nicole Givens Kurtz

The Portal Guards by Marcia Colette

Moses: The Chronicles of Harriet Tubman by Balogun

CHAPTER ONE

Every year, the heroes got younger.

A pale sun hovered above Jeju Island. The eternal breeze swept humid air across the hills in a high-pitched, keening wail. Jeong Seok gazed down at his son, Ha Jun. His shadow cloaked the young man in darkness as Ha Jun meditated in the courtyard, his legs folded beneath him, back straight, eyes closed. Sweat soaked his naked chest crisscrossed with old scars.

Jeong Seok clasped his hands behind his back and barked out, "Ha Jun!"

His son's eyes flicked open. "Father?"

"I petitioned the governor for a quest." Jeong Seok studied Ha Jun. When he didn't get a reaction from his son, he continued, "The governor accepted today. You've been assigned an adventure."

Ha Jun's eyes narrowed. Jeong Seok tensed, noting his son's tell. To others, that slight gesture would appear insignificant. To Jeong Seok, it was a curse of disapproval that his son roared at him.

"You are displeased at this opportunity?" Jeong Seok asked.

"No, Father," Ha Jun responded with his face blank.

Jeong Seok saw through the polite mask and curled the hand behind his back into a fist. "Do you understand how difficult it was for me to secure this quest for you?"

"Yes, Father."

"How many favors I traded to get my request to the governor before any others?"

"Yes, Father," Ha Jun said, voice flat and emotionless.

"And you respond to me like that?" *The insolence!* A quiver ran through Jeong Seok, and he darted forward and struck his son in the chest.

The boy didn't flinch, but simply murmured, "I apologize, Father."

Despite himself, pride welled in Jeong Seok's chest. The blow had been hard, but Ha Jun's muscles had the density of stone. Striking him left Jeong Seok's knuckles throbbing with pain.

"You have trained diligently, son. I appreciate your effort." Jeong Seok rested his palm on Ha Jun's shoulder. "I will go to your uncle for the horses now. Get ready. We leave to Jeju-si the moment I return."

Ha Jun picked up his sword and stood. Simply carrying the glyph blade took years of intense strength conditioning of the arms. Jeong Seok marveled that Ha Jun could carry the sword with ease now. Ha Jun walked to the smallest of several short brick dwellings and went inside to prepare for the journey.

Jeong Seok nodded, satisfied. He left the courtyard and turned left down the dirt lane that cut through the orange trees. Over the years, Jeong Seok had signed contracts with several merchants who shipped his oranges to Il-Bon, Jung-Guk, and other lands across the ocean. He should be a wealthy man, and most islanders thought him to be. They didn't know how far in debt the glyph sword had placed him. Ha Jun's children, grandchildren, and great-grandchildren would be paying for the weapon if Ha Jun didn't become a hero.

Jeong Seok's older brother, Gwang Min, ran the shipping arm of their family business and had a herd of Jeju's finest horses. Jeong Seok passed from under the orange trees and walked around an olleh, one of the big hills dotting the island. On the other side of the olleh, a wooden gate encircled a wide swath of flat land. Inside, horses ate grass and lay in the shade to avoid the hot sun.

He swung open the gate, and the nearest horses looked up at him, their tails flicking. He followed a well-trodden path that cut across the field to several stone brick homes with thatched roofs. The wooden door to the widest one stood open. Jeong Seok paused at the threshold and called out, "Older brother? Are you inside?"

"Jeong Seok?" His brother stepped into the inner room. A stout man with broad, muscular arms and legs, Gwang Min was known around the island as an honest man with a bright smile. Jeong Seok had dealt with his older brother's upstanding ideals his entire life, and he knew he had to manage this request carefully to avoid a disagreement with him.

"I wasn't expecting you," Gwang Min said. "What brings you here today?"

"I apologize for disturbing you." He bowed. "Were you busy?"

"My wife's restaurant is hosting a wedding party

tonight. We're slaughtering a horse this afternoon to provide the guests with the freshest meat possible."

Good, Jeong Seok thought. He had caught his brother on a busy day, which meant that Gwang Min would be more interested in getting back to work than asking too many questions.

"Then I won't keep you. I need to borrow two horses."

Gwang Min nodded. "Are you taking Ha Jun on a trip?"

"I am."

"Come back tomorrow and they'll be ready for you." Gwang Min stepped out of the doorway into the sunlight. "The bride and grooms' families live in Seongsan. They need to be picked up and brought here. Our travel horses will all be put to use to pull the carriages."

"We can take any that are available. They don't have to be your strongest," Jeong Seok said.

"You think I'll allow my younger brother to ride around Jeju on any but my best steed?" Gwang Min laughed. "I'm running a business, Jeong Seok. What would the villagers say if they saw you on a fat mare better meant for slaughter than riding?"

Gwang Min was right, of course. Customers got the horse they could afford, but when Jeong Seok's oranges were transported from the farm to the market or the harbor, his brother only supplied him the broadest, most handsome steeds whose newly brushed coats had a glossy sheen.

Still, Jeong Seok didn't have time to wait.

"Forgive me, older brother, but I have important business today. This short notice is unforgivable, and I don't enjoy putting you in this position. We do not need your best horses, which should be used for the wedding. Loan us any two so that we can go on our way immediately."

His older brother watched him, a frown budding to replace his smile. Jeong Seok met Gwang Min's eye and then glanced away.

"Has something happened?" Gwang Min asked. "Why the sudden urgency to travel?"

Jeong Seok kept his face impassive as he ran a series of excuses through his mind. Now his older brother was asking questions. Gwang Min could be as stubborn as his horses, and just as tireless when he set his sight on something.

"I will take Ha Jun to the governor. He's been assigned a quest," Jeong Seok said.

Even without meeting his brother's gaze, the sharp intake of breath told Jeong Seok of his brother's disapproval.

"He's not even seventeen yet," Gwang Min exclaimed. "This is madness!"

"The heroes are getting younger," Jeong Seok shot back, spittle flying from his mouth.

"And so are the corpses," Gwang Min replied. "Fathers are sending their sons off before they're ready, and funeral mounds are springing up in the countryside like weeds."

Jeong Seok wiped his lips and snorted. "Don't compare my son to those failures. Ha Jun is the strongest boy on the island. He's won every fighting competition since he was a child. He can run for days and is faster than your racing horses. His skill with the sword is unmatched by any other, soldier or villager."

"Yes, the boy is gifted. You've pushed him past any

sane level of endurance, and, amazingly, the boy still lives." Gwang Min leaned toward Jeong Seok and lowered his voice. "I know where those scars on his body come from, Little Brother, and they weren't from the regional competitions."

Jeong Seok's face burned at the accusation. "The evils that heroes must face out there — the dangers — how do you think they prepare for them? How do you think they survive the challenges except by being pushed to their limits and beyond? What do you think it takes to journey into a serpent's lair and slay it? Do you think the man-eating tigers of Gangwon-do allow for mistakes? They consume weakness just as they feast upon the flesh of young men!"

"Don't lecture me on things I already know," Gwang Min said. "The evils of the world devour the weakness of man, and only the greatest of us ever become heroes. But that's why it's best to wait until Ha Jun has matured."

"No!" Jeong Seok struggled to hold the violence alive inside of himself in check. "Who is a man in this world if they don't make a name for themselves? Who will remember them after they're dead? Who will sing their praises?"

"Younger brother," Gwang Min said, his face hard, "Ha Jun does not need to throw away his life to be known. Look at you! You're already known in Jeju, the mainland, and countries beyond."

"For oranges!" Jeong Seok's shriek rattled him, and Gwang Min's eyes narrowed. "I want more for Ha Jun. I want his name to be sung from the lips of women. I want his exploits to make other men jealous, to make them dream of what they could accomplish one day if they were

only strong enough. You've never understood, older brother. This domestic life was enough for you. A wife, children, a ranch, the horses. This was all you ever needed, but I always wanted to become more."

"You could have been more," Gwang Min said in a hushed, matter-of-fact voice.

"When?" Jeong Seok demanded of him. "After the war in the north when we were conscripted? After we came back here to take over the family's farm and ranch? After we were married off? After we had children? After the days became months, and the months became years? You and I, we fought and distinguished ourselves amongst our peers. But the Emperor got all of the glory. Then we came back home. We took over our father's businesses and raised families of our own. And look where we are now. Who will remember our names?"

"Our children. And our children's children."

"And then who? In a hundred years, who will speak the names of Kang Jeong Seok and Kang Gwang Min?"

"In a hundred years?" Gwang Min frowned. "What difference does that make?"

"What difference does it make to be known? To become legends? You can stand here and ask me what difference that makes?" Jeong Seok cast his gaze up at the sky. Beyond the clouds, higher than the horizon, the stars dwelt.

"You won't stop me, older brother," Jeong Seok said without looking back down at Gwang Min. "I will take Ha Jun to the governor, and he will go on the quest that has been assigned to him."

"And if I went to the governor and told him that this was a mistake?"

Jeong Seok relaxed at his brother's naïve threat. Gwang Min couldn't grasp the competitive spirit to be better than one's peers. The governor needed heroes from Jeju to distinguish themselves on the mainland. Like Jeong Seok, the governor craved greatness of Jeju's citizens so that the reputation of the small island at the southernmost tip of South Hanguk would increase on the mainland. In the past, many concerned family members had tried to stop young men from taking a quest but had failed. It was Ha Jun's decision, and once the papers were signed, nothing could stop him.

"If you refuse to lend us a horse, you will slow us down, but you will not stop us." Jeong Seok met Gwang Min's gaze at last, and the two brothers glared at each other.

"If I give my nephew only an extra hour among the living, so be it." Gwang Min turned to head back into the house. "Here, at least, your request has been denied. Goodbye, Younger Brother."

CHAPTER TWO

Ha Jun spied his father, who walked at a quick pace down the path threading through the trees. Unsuppressed rage contorted his face, and Ha Jun's heartbeat quickened. He focused to stop the agitation working its way through him and managed to push it down. There, the vibrating ball of terror remained tucked away and tethered: harmless.

"Ha Jun!" The word erupted from his father's mouth, and Ha Jun ran to meet him at the edge of the courtyard. "You are ready."

The tone didn't sound like his father had posed a question. Confused, Ha Jun struggled for the best way to respond. If he hesitated too long, it would be as bad as saying the wrong thing.

"I have packed my travel bag." He indicated the leather pouch slung on his back and held up his sword. "I am prepared to leave immediately." He looked beyond his father at the path leading from the farm. "Will Uncle provide the horses?"

His father threw him a hard glare. Ha Jun buried a flinch and maintained a relaxed posture. Opponents studied each other for weakness. The projection of strength was key to winning a battle. He had learned this from his father, who had not hesitated to exploit Ha Jun's mistakes during their years of training.

"Your aunt has a wedding reception to host today," his father said, his body rigid. "My brother needs them for her guests. He cannot spare mounts for us."

Ha Jun pondered the news. His uncle had horses on the ranch to pull carriages and wagons, to race, and for consumption. How could he possibly not have two to spare?

"Is there a problem?" His father studied him.

Ha Jun kept his breathing even as he wondered how his father always knew his thoughts. It was as if he read his mind like he read official scrolls.

"No, Father," Ha Jun answered.

His father laid a heavy hand on his shoulder, and Ha Jun suppressed the instinctive urge to recoil at the touch that usually delivered pain, not comfort. For several moments his father stared at him, and Ha Jun tensed his muscles to absorb a surprise blow, a technique his father had employed often to keep him on his toes. The enemy calculated with the intent to kill, and Ha Jun could never let his guard down.

"You are not a child of destiny," his father said, and the words struck Ha Jun harder than any blow. "You are a boy, no more than a farmer's son."

Ha Jun's eyes dropped to the knotted grass of the courtyard. So, it had all been pointless. The exhaustive training, the deadly combat lessons, the blood that had

often stained his clothes, the nights he'd sobbed in pain from a body pushed beyond its limits. Why had he endured all of that since before he could remember if his father didn't believe he was meant for greatness?

His father tightened his grip on Ha Jun's shoulder. "And do you know what you should say to those who tell you that are only a farmer's son? You must say, 'Who cares?' It is up to us to fashion our fate as we desire. It is up to us to forge our own destinies. The gods help those who help themselves."

Ha Jun jerked to attention and quivered at his father's words. Ha Jun knew the strength of his arms, the power in his legs that had been fostered by his father's brutal training regimen. If the gods didn't help him, could Ha Jun break the obstacles that stood before him with his own might?

"Other fathers on the island, do you know what they want for their children? An ordinary life. To fight in some war where the Emperor gets all of the glory. To come back home to take over the family business. To be married off to some girl. To sire children to take care of them when they are old. That is what other fathers want for their sons. But you will not have that, Ha Jun. You will have more because we have worked your entire life for you to accomplish that goal. You will stand above other men and claim your place amongst the stars."

Ha Jun read such fierce pride in his father's eyes that his heart swelled with love.

"Believe nothing in this life can or will stop you. At this moment, we have no horses, yet you must make it to the other side of Hallasan before the sun falls and the governor's doors close. There is only one way to accomplish this: you must run."

Ha Jun thought back to the many long days during which he'd done just that. Around the wide island, his father at his back on a horse, whip in hand. Each time Ha Jun slowed, a flash of blinding pain would follow the crack of the whip. Blood would run down his bare back and sides. When he was younger, Ha Jun would scream with each blow. When he crashed to the earth out of utter exhaustion, his father would crack the whip over and over, and Ha Jun would writhe on the sandy shores of Jeju until he finally struggled back to his feet to keep on.

As he grew older, he stopped crying out at the lash. Sometimes, he'd slow on purpose just to prove that he could take the blow. Like the terror, he kept the pain locked away, a ball of energy that vibrated at a low hum deep inside of him.

Ha Jun met his father's gaze, who seemed to see the memories that played in his thoughts.

"Every moment of every day of training had a purpose," he said to Ha Jun. "Now run, with all you have been given, and reach the governor's house before night falls."

Ha Jun bowed at his father's command, and his father returned the gesture. Then his father stepped forward and shoved Ha Jun out of the courtyard.

"I said, 'Run'!"

His father held no whip, but Ha Jun still felt a phantom blow to his back. He darted forward, through the orange trees, around the olleh, and past his uncle's ranch. Horses were spread out across the wide field, their heads bent low as they chewed on grass. Ha Jun considered asking his uncle for one of the mounts but thought better of it. His father had already tried, and if he said that it couldn't be done, then it must be impossible.

Ha Jun heard the gallop of a horse and turned to see his uncle racing towards him on his fastest steed. Perhaps circumstances had changed. Ha Jun slowed but did not stop. A sword dangled from his uncle's saddle, and Ha Jun wondered if he rode armed because he carried important cargo.

"Nephew." His uncle caught up to Ha Jun and cantered beside him. "Stop a moment and take a rest with me in the house."

Ha Jun looked at the sun's position in the sky. His trek over the inactive volcano, Hallasan, would take at least six hours if he walked. Going around the volcano added two hours. Sprinting would cut the trip in half, equaling the same amount of time it would take on horseback. None on the island could dash over the volcano as Ha Jun could on his powerful legs, but a horseback ride would make the journey easier.

Ha Jun glanced at the horses on the ranch again, then at his uncle. Something didn't feel right. His father had worked hard to have Ha Jun selected for a quest. If a horse was available, why would he not have brought it back with him immediately after the visit to his uncle? And why did his uncle's serious expression seem like a grimace today?

"Uncle, I apologize." He bowed slightly without pausing in his steady stride. "I have no time to rest. I must make it to Jeju-si, and I have a long way yet to go."

"I demand that you stop." His uncle kicked the horse. The animal jumped forward and got in front of Ha Jun, who sidestepped it and darted off faster to put some distance between himself and his uncle. He didn't understand what was going on, but he knew nothing should stop him from his arrival to Jeju-si, even if the delay was caused by family.

"What's wrong with you, Nephew, that you would disobey me? You've always been a respectful boy."

Throughout his childhood, his uncle had been kind to him, and had given him silver coins for Children's Day and Chuseok. When his uncle hunted in Hallasan Forest, he always brought back strips of venison for Ha Jun and gave him horse meat to keep him strong as he endured the long training sessions that his father demanded. His uncle had always protected him, but ultimately, he was not his father, and Ha Jun sensed that if he didn't make it to the governor's house in time, if he missed the departure of the quest, he would never be able to return home again.

Ha Jun said, "Please allow me to use a mount so that I can make it across the mountain easier."

Frustration curled his uncle's face. "This is madness!" With a deft movement, he released the sword from its sheath and held the point to Ha Jun's neck.

"You will come back to the house, Nephew, and we will talk."

The threat sunk into Ha Jun and went deep to disturb that condensed ball of terror, anger, and pain he kept pent up inside. The energy pulsated and surged out to fill him. A crimson hue colored the world as the vibration of emotions choked off further considerations. Ha Jun snaked beneath the blade, leapt forward, and punched the horse in the head. A crack echoed from the blow as its skull cratered. The horse collapsed with a violent neigh.

His uncle could not leap away in time as the steed rolled on its side and crushed his leg. His moans floated to Ha Jun, and he called for help to be freed from the heavy animal pinning him to the earth.

Ha Jun would not be deterred further, however. Without a backwards glance, he dug the balls of his feet into the earth and sprinted towards Mount Hallasan.

CHAPTER THREE

Windshine was tired of watching young men die. Of the four that she'd gone to the mainland with on this last journey, the Dark Elf had managed to bring back the remains of only one.

The deck hands carried Ji Hun's bloody body down the gangway, his head flopping on his shredded neck. They laid him in the carriage that had come to transport Windshine back to the governor's office and covered the body with a shroud.

She walked down the gangway and stepped onto the wooden docks. When the deck hands spat at her feet, she stared straight ahead, her arms folded, her gloved hands tucked into the red sleeves of her deel. The carriage driver, a governor's employee named Yeong Tae, met the ferry captain at the end of the gangway.

"Careful with her," the captain growled, motioning to Windshine. "Her kind's cursed."

Yeong Tae said nothing as he slipped the captain a

silver coin, then went back to the carriage and gestured for Windshine to climb up beside him on the perch.

"We shouldn't linger," Yeong Tae said. He watched the crowd gathered at Jeju-si's western port with a wary eye. With a flick of the reins, he set the horses moving at a steady pace down the lane, cutting through the docks.

"Rumors about you have been spreading amongst the people," Yeong Tae said. His sword lay sheathed next to him in the carriage. "There's been talk of revenge by the locals. And murder."

Their anger was misplaced, but the people saw her as an easier target than the real evils wandering the country. Windshine had no sword, and carried no visible weapon, but Elvish words of magic were woven into the fabric of her round black hat with a blue domed top, her sky blue tunic with long red sleeves, and her soft orange boots. The fingerless gloves covered with silver fur could be used to kill dozens under the right circumstances. Windshine was well protected. The people of the island posed little danger to her, even in large numbers, so a murder plot wasn't her main concern. The greater risk would be if she were to harm, or accidentally kill, a human. The Dark Elves had lived a precarious existence in the land of South Hanguk since they arrived on its shores four hundred years ago. The death of a human by one of them would turn the citizens against her compatriots living in the country. No one wanted war, especially the Dark Elves that sought only peace.

"What happened on the mainland?" Yeong Tae asked. He inclined his head towards the back of the carriage. "How did they die this time?"

"They died trying to become heroes." Windshine spoke

quietly so that her words wouldn't be overheard. Humans lived such short lives, and some became obsessed with shining brightly in the brief moment they existed. She didn't want to think about the young men's failed expedition, but Yeong Tae liked to hear the exploits of those who went on quests. He himself would never undertake one. He didn't have the motivation to be anything more than a normal inhabitant of Jeju. But he was still curious, and through the words she wove, he could live vicariously through the fortunes, and misfortunes, of others.

Ultimately, Windshine was a storyteller to the humans, a way for those who settled for a simple life to still find excitement in the adventures of others. So she fulfilled her duty as decreed by the Emperors of South Hanguk to the long-lived Dark Elves. She told Yeong Tae the story of the tiger.

TEN DAYS AGO, she met four prospective heroes at the governor's office in Jeju. Their quest had been clear enough. A man-eating tiger had wandered down from Seoraksan Mountain and had settled close to the town of Sokcho in Gangwan-do Province. The citizens of Sokcho soon discovered men, women and children torn apart and partially consumed on farms surrounding the town. The mayor had no fighters who could handle the beast, so he declared an emergency and petitioned the Emperor for special forces that could hunt down the tiger and kill it.

Word spread throughout the regions of South Hanguk that skilled fighters with the courage to slay the beast could make a name for themselves. The governor of Jeju lobbied furiously to have warriors from the island selected for the quest. When the appeal was granted, the governor's aides quickly went through the dossier of eligible young men. Since Jeju was at the southernmost tip of the country, any warriors sent from the island would have to travel farther to Gangwon-do in the distant north of South Hanguk than the ones who started from closer regions. The governor hastily chose four young men from the list of applicants that his aides recommended and wasted no time in giving them supplies and sending them on their way so that they could beat the competition to the glory of a kill. The long-lived Dark Elf would accompany them to record the exploits of their grand adventure.

The journey started like many others that Windshine had taken. The trip by ferry from Jeju to the port of Busan on the mainland took half a day. The four warriors disembarked, rented horses, and began the three-day trip to Gangwon-do. The companions got along well at first. The youngest, Min-Ho, was eighteen. The oldest, Ji Hun, was twenty-five. They didn't speak to Windshine and watched her as they would a foreboding shadow trailing after them. They reached Gangwon-do on the afternoon of the third day, and Sokcho on the morning of the fourth. The mayor greeted them and told them that other groups of adventurers had arrived and had already begun the hunt. Ji Hun asked if they'd come too late.

"No one has come back yet," the mayor had responded, so the boys refilled their provisions and started toward Seoraksan Mountains.

Then it began to rain.

Dark clouds hovered menacingly above them, and the craggy peaks of the rocky mountains became lost from view. Lightning struck the ground as if the sky battled against her brother, earth. The land became mud, and a flash flood surged down the canyon and wiped away Min-Ho. The other three fought to save him while Windshine watched from where she clung to a sturdy tree. Ultimately, their efforts proved fruitless.

The company became dispirited and cast dark glances towards the Dark Elf as if it was somehow all her fault. Hours later, Min-Ho found his way back to camp without his horse. They cheered and thanked the ancestral spirits for bringing the company back together again.

Windshine stared at the bedraggled figure covered in mud and said nothing.

When finally reaching Seoraksan, the company camped in the forest and discussed a strategy to track, trap, and kill the tiger. They had not seen signs of the groups that had preceded them and concluded that the quest hadn't yet been completed. Being as close to danger as they were, the group set up a perimeter and decided they would sleep in shifts of two in three-hour intervals.

That night, one of the four men vanished on his watch. When no tracks were found, the other three companions plunged deeper into the forest surrounding Seoraksan in search of him. All day they looked for him as the sun rose into the sky and the air became hot under its steady gaze. Later, when the sun set, the company, exhausted, sweaty and discouraged, again made camp. They fell into an argument amongst themselves, as some thought they should spread out further to make better use of their time, and others thought they should remain closer to where he had disappeared. Being no closer to their actual goal of killing the tiger, it worried them that there was no sign of the companies of young men that had entered the forest first.

The next morning, another of their group vanished, leaving only Min-Ho and Ji Hun, who got into a fierce argument. Ji Hun insisted that they leave. Windshine hung back from them, watchful, as no one had asked for her advice, and seemed unaware of her as they tried to convince the other of the wisdom of their decision. Finally, Ji Hun cursed Min-Ho and said, "Go to your death, then. My quest is over."

Ji Hun grabbed his pack, slung it around his shoulder, and stuck his swords back into his hanbok. When he turned to start back down the path through the forest, a wide, feral smile spread over Min-Ho's face. His teeth elongated into fangs with a deep growl. Ji Hun spun around, and the shapeshifting tiger leapt at him and ripped out his throat before he could draw his weapon. The beast didn't hesitate to turn its sights on Windshine next, and sprang at her, his hands growing long claws.

Attacking the Dark Elf was the man-eating tiger's only mistake.

"IT'S TRAGIC," Yeong Tae said, and gave the covered body behind them a solemn nod. "He wasn't ready, though. But then, so many of them aren't, are they?" He sighed. "The weeping of his mother will haunt their village tonight."

The carriage left the docks behind and entered Jeju-si. The one-story stone buildings with thatched roofs leaned against each other in the crowded city. Narrow alleys snaked away from the main road running through Jeju-si.

People sat on short wooden benches in front of shops that sold fruits and meats and seafood, household items and fabrics. Sweaty children in loose pants and shirts studied their subjects from lessons scratched into wide leaves of parchment tied together with twine. Men smoking long pipes exuding sweet smelling tobacco and women carrying babies on their backs or baskets on their heads stared at the carriage as it passed. Their hostile gazes floated between Windshine and the dead body in the back.

"Don't worry," Yeong Tae said. "They know you're under the protection of the governor."

Windshine didn't relax. Her soul had grown fatigued, and she desired a rest from accompanying the prospective heroes on their quests. She was lonely and longed to speak to her people scattered throughout South Hanguk. There had been less than twenty-five of them that had arrived in South Hanguk several centuries ago. The Emperor had recognized their great power and decided to both use them to give his nation an advantage, but also to separate them so that they couldn't pose a threat to his throne. Windshine had been separated from her sister, Blythe, and hadn't seen her since being sent to Jeju.

There was only one other Dark Elf on the island, who taught high-level spells on Mount Hallasan. It was another woman, as the Emperor had also decreed to keep the male Dark Elves separate from the female Dark Elves so that they could not sire children. Windshine thought it was time she and her counterpart switched roles on the island, since her counterpart did not have to travel on quests and could spend all of her time teaching human pupils. However, Windshine wasn't a genius at spell casting, and only excelled at crafting magic items.

The next quest shouldn't come for a month or two. Windshine decided to discuss her retirement with the governor's office. Too many evils existed to wreak havoc in this country, and humans were simply not producing the caliber of man needed to vanquish them.

The steeple roof of the governor's office rose above all the other buildings of Jeju-si. The guards waved Yeong Tae through the tall, spiked gates, their eyes lingering on Ji Hun's ravaged body. The horses clattered across the neatly cut stone blocks to the governor's office. When Yeong Tae pulled the reins to stop them, Windshine stood to hop off.

"It's not your fault," Yeong Tae insisted, the tenderness he felt for her exposed in the way he stared at her. He leaned towards her as if he wished to wrap her in his arms and protect her from the dangers of the world.

Nearing a thousand years old, Windshine viewed all humans as newborns. She had already ascertained Yeong Tae's growing infatuation with her. He seemed to desire that they become more intimate, but in him she only saw the young boy who used to wait on the docks with his father in this very carriage. She remembered Yeong Tae's grief when his father passed away a year ago, and how he lacked confidence when he had had to take over the reins of the family business.

Windshine never asked any questions of him, having seen everything humans had to offer. Except for regaling him as was her duty, she rarely responded to the personal questions he occasionally asked to get to know her better. In his early twenties, Yeong Tae would soon be married and start a family of his own. This attraction he had for her would evaporate in the face of the responsibilities of being a husband and a father.

Without another word to him, Windshine hopped down from the perch and walked towards the governor's hall. She abruptly stopped at the sight before her, her heart sinking with sadness.

Three new young men stood in front of the governor's chair, their faces full of excitement. Windshine couldn't stand to look at them and turned back to the gates as thoughts of simply fleeing flittered through her mind. Again, she came to a sudden stop, her eyes widening at the strange sight of a boy in his mid-teens racing down the dirt lane towards the governor's house. Her heart skipped a beat at his incredible speed, the strength in his legs propelling him forward like a typhoon. People standing in front of the buildings lining the main city lane turned to look at him, their mouths dropping open as he shot by them. Windshine perceived energy vibrating in him, a compacted ball of power threatening to explode and rip the boy apart.

Her knees became weak, her skin flushed. When he sped by her, she submitted to a compulsion to reach out and run the tips of her fingers along his muscular, sweaty arm. He glanced at her, and for a moment their gazes locked, and reality ceased to exist. Then time leapt forward, and he was bounding up the steps to take his place as the fourth of a doomed band of young mortals.

CHAPTER FOUR

In his sixteen years, a woman had never touched Ha Jun like that. The way the tips of her fingers brushed against his arm sent a thrill through him. For that moment, time vanished, and the world fell away such that all in existence was only this woman staring at him.

She didn't wear the customary hanbok. Instead, her foreign robes flowed over her slender figure like ocean waves. Her round black hat completely covered her hair, and though he couldn't see it at this moment, Ha Jun was sure that it would be as unique as the rest of her appearance.

Despite the heat, she wore fingerless fur gloves. Her velvet skin absorbed the sunlight. Her strange attire and dark hue wasn't what most captured Ha Jun's attention. In that moment frozen in time, he saw every detail of her eyes, the sky blue corneas, the irises bright brown and shifting like sand. With those strange orbs, she gazed at him and through him to some hidden place deep inside of himself.

The impression of her touch lingered upon his arm even after he'd passed her. It invaded his skin, set his blood on fire, and pumped like a toxin to his chest. A violent tension clutched his heart, and a desire birthed inside of him to stay in that timeless moment so that he could gaze upon her forever.

Ha Jun faltered, but his father's brutal training focused his wayward thoughts. He quickly remembered where he was and what he was meant to do even as the heart in his scarred chest sought to distract him. He pushed the tension down and tore his attention away from her. He took the stairs to the governor's chair several at a time and stopped beside three young men. They turned to stare at his sudden entrance. Ha Jun stood before them, sweating and breathing hard. The governor had not yet arrived, but an aide in official garb stood at the chair, and Ha Jun bowed to him.

"I apologize for being late," he said between breaths. "I apologize for my messy appearance." He bowed again, and beads of sweat dripped off him.

The official wore a loose, cream colored hanbok with the governor's insignia on its sleeves. Distaste at Ha Jun's abrupt entrance wrinkled his face beneath the black conical hat with a wide rim perched on his head. Despite the open platform of the governor's office, Ha Jun became distinctly aware of his own musky smell after running for so long. The official pointed to a basin and cloth at the edge of the office.

"Clean your face before the governor comes," he instructed, his voice cool, "and be quick about it. He will arrive any moment now."

Ha Jun nodded and darted to the basin in the corner.

Out of the corner of his eye, he saw the woman in the courtyard staring at him. He also felt the gaze of the official and the three other young men, and his hands shook as he took up the cloth. He dipped it in the water and wiped off his forehead, cheeks, and chin, the water dripping down his neck into his collar. When he reached over to wring out the towel, he accidentally knocked over the basin. The water spilled across the floor and down the steps. Snickers sounded from the men behind him, and Ha Jun flushed. Of course, the woman's attention remained on him.

Ha Jun's heartbeat quickened, his teeth clenching so hard that it hurt his gums. He stopped breathing, and the words *Stupid, Stupid, Stupid* played in his head. He wanted to reach out and right the overturned basin, but the ball of energy inside of him flooded him to the point that his muscles became rigid. The crimson rage offered only ridicule instead of decisive action this time and burned him with his blunders. He was a fool, too clumsy to become a hero. He would fail his father. If he left the island on a quest, he would fail the governor. He would live in shame for the rest of his life, and in his shame, he would hide himself away from the world to die alone. He wasn't ready.

You are ready!

His father's words cut through him like a lash. Ha Jun struggled to emerge out of the doubt. Hadn't his father always believed in him? Isn't that why he had pushed him so relentlessly? Would his father have wasted his time had he not known that his son could stand among the stars and become a hero?

Ha Jun exhaled sharply. He focused on the panic and

forced it back down until it merged with the vibrating ball of energy again, tucked away and tethered inside of himself.

I am ready!

Ha Jun reached out and righted the basin. He wiped the water from his face, laid the cloth beside the basin, and stood. He glimpsed the governor, personal guards, and several other aides approaching the stairs. Ha Jun joined the three young men, who stood straighter as the governor climbed the steps.

The governor wore a blood red hanbok with a black and white collar and silk slippers. A black rimless hat with a tall bamboo cone sat on his head. The ends of his thin, gray mustache pointed down to his long gray beard. Ha Jun had never been in the presence of the governor before, but he'd been regaled by tales of his adventures, and stood in awe of him now. All governors throughout South Hanguk had earned the reputation of being a hero at some time in their past. They were fierce warriors, the best of their generation.

The young men bowed low as the governor took the chair in the center of the hall. The official stepped forward and said, "Please, introduce yourselves one at a time."

The first to step forward had two swords and a dagger on his hip, as well as a fire lance, the barrel carved into a dragon's head, slung on his shoulder. "I am Seong Min," he said, "and I am twenty-six years old."

Seong Min stepped back, and the second stepped forward. He only had a small dagger at his waist, but he wore the gray robes of a monk and a golden pendant of a three-legged crow around his neck. "I am Su Won, and I am twenty-three years old."

Su Won stepped back, and the third stepped forward. He wore golden scale armor, the only one of them to do so. At his side, he carried two swords and a dagger strapped to his leg. "I am Yeong-Su, and I am twenty years old."

Yeong-Su stepped back, and Ha Jun stepped forward.

"I am Ha Jun, and I am sixteen years old."

Seong Min, Su Won, and Yeong-Su gasped at Ha Jun's age. They turned to gape at him.

Before anything more could be said, the governor nodded. "Welcome, young warriors and future heroes! Of all the people on Jeju Island, none are as strong or capable as you who stand before me now. The journey before you will be fraught with difficulties, but you must stand fast. With courageous hearts, you will overcome any obstacle that stands in your way. Your fate has been written in the stars. You are the children of destiny!"

Seong Min, Su Won, and Yeong-Su stood rigid, pride shining in their faces. Seong Min withdrew his sword and saluted the governor. Su Won and Yeong-Su quickly followed suit. Ha Jun, confused by the gesture, hesitated a moment before sliding his glyph sword from its sheath and clumsily copying their salute.

The governor motioned to one of the officials, who removed a scroll from a pouch at his side and handed it to the governor. The governor read in silence for several moments. A bright smile lit his face.

"Truly, you four are fortunate! A grand adventure has come your way, a quest that will rival even the ones I partook in before any of you were even born. How I envy you for this glorious chance at greatness!"

The four young men turned to each other. Eager grins

split their faces. The official cleared his throat so that they would stand at attention again.

"In Jellonam-do Province, the city of Suncheon is under siege." The governor paused, and the young men leaned closer in anticipation.

"An ak-ma has taken refuge in Naganeupseong Fortress beyond Jukdobong Forest."

"An ak-ma," Seong Min breathed out with excitement. "We will go to destroy an ak-ma!"

Ha Jun stared at him, confused. His father had taught him about ak-ma. Voracious demons who devoured the souls of man, they were some of the most feared creatures of South Hanguk. The cursed chanced upon one with great misfortune, and only the foolish challenged and attempted to defeat the ak-ma, for little brought misery and death faster than a demon.

"Tomorrow you will take the ferry to Nokdong on the mainland," the governor said. "You will be accompanied by the recorder of tales."

The governor directed his attention to the left, and the young men followed his gaze. The strange woman had joined them in the governor's office without being noticed. Seong Min, Su Won, and Yeong-Su stiffened at her presence, their faces hardening. The thrill from before shook Ha Jun again, and the feel of her fingertips along his arm played in his mind. The foreignness of her strange blue and brown eyes disturbed him, but something else, an unrelenting attraction that radiated through his body, drew him to her.

The woman bowed. "I am Windshine. I will be the recorder of tales for your adventure."

Her accent elongated the Hangugeo syllables, her

tongue rolling them out from her mouth so that it sounded as if she was singing instead of speaking. Beside Ha Jun, the young men twisted their faces in disgust. Ha Jun didn't know what he should think. Hangugeo sounded beautiful with her accent, but her pronunciation was completely wrong and struck him as strange in its twisting of their language.

"When I am done composing stories of your brave deeds," Windshine said, "future generations will forever remember your names among the greatest heroes this country has ever known."

The governor stood. "You will commence on your journey tomorrow. The ferry has already been arranged, and you will be given a generous stipend to start you on your quest. Rest well, young warriors!"

The four young men bowed repeatedly as the governor made his way back down the stairs and across the stone courtyard.

"Can you believe our luck?" Yeong-Su said. "Before we're done, we'll be the stuff of myth."

Ha Jun tried to smile, but worry at the danger they faced made it impossible for him to behave as confident as the others.

Seong Min noticed his unease and laid a hand on Ha Jun's shoulder. "Don't worry, Little Brother. We're the sons of legend."

The three companions ignored the Dark Elf that hovered near them. They broke into a rousing cheer, and Ha Jun joined them. Perhaps they were right, he thought as he sung along. Perhaps they truly were the stuff of prophecy. He imagined returning to his father in a few short days, the slayer of a demon and a hero of South Hanguk.

Standing beside the other young men, he forgot the anxiety, terror, and anger tethered inside of him, vibrating with a life of their own.

CHAPTER FIVE

Seong Min quieted the young men and turned to the official he had met when he first arrived at the governor's office. Bowing, he said, "I will take the stipend and buy the supplies for the trip."

The official nodded and removed a leather purse from his hanbok. "This should last you for two weeks." He handed it to Seong Min. "You must be careful with your finances. The ferry back and forth from the island is already paid for, but if you run out of money while you travel, you will have to make up for the shortages on your own."

Seong Min secured the purse to a hoop on his pants.

"The day has gotten late," the official said. The sun had set, and the first stars had risen in the evening sky. "You will lodge in the nearby jjimjilbang tonight. Get as much rest as you can, for you must rise early to catch the ferry."

The official looked east from whence a strong breeze blew. "Another storm is brewing."

Summer was only weeks old, and South Hanguk was

in the midst of rainy season, which would last for another month. Seong Min hoped the storm would wait until the next evening to arrive so that the ferry would not be delayed. The trip to Nokdong wouldn't take long, but violent winds churning up high waves on the Hanguk Strait could be dangerous, and his companions were young. Especially the sixteen-year-old, Kang Ha Jun.

Seong Min turned to his companions, whom he considered his three younger brothers now. Since he was the oldest, they waited for him to issue the order for their next step.

"We should retire to the jjimjilbang for an early dinner, and then a long rest," he told them. He glanced at the foreigner standing several paces away. She hadn't left with the governor, and she didn't talk with the remaining official. She simply stood there like a shadow, attached to them yet existing in a dark world of her own.

Seong Min had heard of the two Dark Elves who lived on the island. South Hanguk people generally kept their distance from the foreigners. Today was the first time he had seen one of them, and she looked as strange as the rumors made her out to be.

From what Seong Min had been told, the other Dark Elf on Jeju was also female, as well as a magic user with incredible power. Seong Min had no proficiency in spell casting, but even if he did, he wouldn't be able to study with the Dark Elf that lived on Hallasan. Only humans who showed genius level magical talent studied under the Dark Elves. Those exceptionally gifted human mages eventually became aides in the Emperor's court, while lesser spell casters became officials to governors throughout South Hanguk.

How powerful was this Elf? He didn't like her solemn appearance. Even more, he didn't trust her. No one he knew did. All of them found her eyes especially unsettling.

Seong Min had never seen anything quite as alien as her eyes. When she had introduced herself, the sensation of falling a great distance into some different space had overcome him. He had forced himself to focus his sight right beyond her head as he struggled to understand the unusual way she spoke Hangugeo. What had been her name?

Windshine?

The people of South Hanguk considered the Dark Elves to be cursed, and often wondered why the Emperor allowed them to stay in the country. This Windshine seemed like a temptress—her angular face perfectly sculpted, her supple and shapely body beneath her sky blue tunic oddly enticing.

Not knowing what he should do with her, Seong Min decided to ignore her. Motioning to his younger brothers, he started down the steps, and they followed him into the courtyard. They walked to the gates in front of the governor's office. There, several people stood waiting. Seong Min led them to his wife first. She carried their infant son in a podaegi on her back. The boy squealed at his father's approach, and Seong Min pinched his fat cheek.

"Ye-Jin," Seong Min said to his wife, "these are my younger brothers, Su Won, Yeong-Su, and Ha Jun."

Each bowed to her in turn.

"I am happy to meet you for this first time," Ye-Jin said, returning their bows. To her husband, she asked, "You've received your quest? Is it a difficult one?"

"Do you wish me to have an easy one?" Seong Min

said with mock disapproval. He turned to his younger brothers and winked. "My wife wants us to stay safe and secure. She doesn't understand what it takes to be a man."

Ye-Jin rolled her eyes. "Just be careful. Remember that a boy should grow up with his father."

Seong Min leaned in close to his son. "Nothing will ever separate me from you," he promised, and the boy squealed, drool racing down his chin. Seong Min placed his hand on the head of the messy bundle that was his son. He had done many things in his twenty-six years, but nothing would ever be as great as creating this life squirming under his touch.

"To where are you traveling?" Ye-Jin asked.

"Our final destination is Naganeupseong Fortress beyond Jukdobong Forest outside of Suncheon City," he replied. "There's some disturbance there, but don't worry, it's nothing we can't handle."

His wife glanced past her husband, concern spreading over her face. Lowering her voice, she said, "There's been talk that the last group of companions failed. A bloody body came back. Ripped apart so much that his parents could barely recognized him."

With Ye-Jin leaning so close, Seong Min inhaled her bodily scent. Arousal spiked through him. He wished he had time to spend one more night with her in his arms. When he responded to her, his voice had deepened.

"If the journey was easy, there'd be no heroes. If everyone came back alive, there would be no point in going."

Swiftly he darted in and kissed Ye-Jin right beneath her ear. "I will return to you."

"You promise?" she whispered back to him.

Seong Min responded only with a grin before stepping away so that she would not see doubt in his eyes.

"Older Brother," Su Won, standing behind him, said. "Will you meet my mentor?"

Seong Min looked to where a monk stood farther down by the gate and nodded. Clearing his throat, he followed Su Won, and bowed when he reached the monk. The bald-headed mentor bowed back.

After introductions, the monk said, "Su Won will be vital in your fight against the ak-ma. His sword arm is weak, but he is deeply in tune with the ancestral spirits. Protect him when you can but use him as your greatest weapon against the demon when the time is right."

"I promise to take care of him," Seong Min said with a deep bow. "And when the time comes, he will be our instrument of victory."

"Older Brother," Yeong-Su said, "will you meet my parents?"

Seong Min followed his younger brother to his parents and greeted them. He recognized Yeong-Su's father, the mayor of Seogwipo-si in the south. Both Yeong-Su's father and mother wore stylish silk hanbok with the summer colors of blue, yellow and pink dyed on the expensive fabric. His father wore a black hat with a wide brim, and he smoked a long cigarette that emitted a sweet fragrance.

"I am honored to meet you," Seong Min said.

"I am happy that our son has an elder brother such as you in his company," Yeong-Su's father said. "You have the bearing of a solider."

Seong Min nodded. "I was part of the Emperor's force that stormed the mountains of North Hanguk and slew one of the dragons threatening Yang Yang. While I was enlisted, I learned the skill of the fire lance." He tapped the metal tube on his shoulder. "The dragon's lair was heavily guarded by North Hanguk's finest warriors. It was a tough battle, but we prevailed."

"Then my son truly is in good hands," Yeong-Su's father said to his wife. "Seong Min, I believe you to be an honorable and fine man. Correct my son's mistakes. When he is lazy, scold him. When he is brave, encourage him with kind words. By your example, I hope that he learns to be mature in all of his decision making."

After bowing to them again, Seong Min went to Ha Jun. He had not followed them to make introductions, and still stood alongside Seong Min's wife and son.

"Younger Brother," Seong Min said, "I would like to meet your family now. Where are your parents, or older siblings, who came to see you off on your quest?"

Ha Jun seemed to sink into himself. He turned to his left, then to his right, as if each simple movement required great effort. Finally, he opened his mouth, but it took several moments before words came out.

"I am alone."

Seong Min's wife gasped. "No one came to say goodbye and wish you a speedy return? No one in your family cares?"

The baby began to cry, and Seong Min laid a hand on his son's shoulder. He wished his wife hadn't spoken thus and cursed her loose tongue. Ye-Jin had beautiful lips, but sometimes they flapped too much.

"You live on the other side of the island, do you not?" Seong Min asked. "I'm sure they were busy and wish they could be here with you now."

"But no one in his family came," Ye-Jin pointed out again. "How's that possible?"

Seong Min stepped away from his son and stood with Su Won and Yeong-Su. "You are wrong, my love," he corrected his wife. "His brothers are standing right here, exactly where they need to be."

Seong Min extended his hand, and Su Won placed his hand on top, and Yeong-Su placed his hand on top of Su Won's. They stared at Ha Jun, and the tension dissolved as he laid his hand on top of Yeong-Su's. The baby's cries grew louder as a damp wind blew from the east with a loud, piercing wail. In the shadows of the darkening evening, the Dark Elf stood, watching with her strange blue and brown eyes.

CHAPTER SIX

The yellow scale armor had grown heavy. Yeong-Su had been wearing it since dawn, and in the summer heat, he had been sweating beneath it all day. There had only been the briefest respite when he had shed it to wipe off his body and face before entering the governor's office.

"You must project dignity when you stand before the governor," his father had said. "Rules and adherence to proper protocols. Those are the rituals of a future politician. The other men will be commoners, but you are an official's son."

His companions had looked rough, but none more so than Ha Jun, who looked like he'd run all the way to the governor's office right off the farm. Dangers existed everywhere on these quests, and Yeong-Su couldn't imagine an inexperienced sixteen-year-old surviving for long. Adventures were for men. Yeong-Su would do what he could to protect Ha Jun, but he wouldn't lay down his life to save a boy. Ha Jun shouldn't be there.

"We need to sleep soon," their elder brother, Song Seong Min, said. "The jjimjilbang isn't far."

The companions said their last goodbyes to their families, then walked across the lane to a two-story wooden building with a steeple roof. The foreigner followed them. Yeong-Su didn't know how they were supposed to acknowledge her. His father had taught him about the foreigners. He explained that the Elves had been granted the right to remain in South Hanguk generations ago. Supposedly, they were immigrants fleeing a war in their home country. Few beyond the most learned scholars in the capital knew the ancient history of the foreigners. However, everyone knew that the Dark Elves had to pledge loyalty to each new Emperor. They toiled in his service, as well as in the service of the provinces' governors.

The Dark Elves, though cursed and untrustworthy, should be treated as official retainers. However, the foreigner, with her blue and brown eyes, wasn't human, and the correct way to be polite to her escaped Yeong-Su. So he waited for Seong Min to lead the way in proper etiquette, but his older brother seemed unsure around the foreigner, too. Seong Min didn't look at her and didn't speak to her. Yeong-Su decided that for now, the most prudent thing he could do was ignore her, also.

Two doors marked the jjimjilbang's entrance, one with a sign for men, another for women. Yeong-Su felt noticeable relief spread throughout the group now that they had the opportunity to separate themselves from the foreigner. The four of them entered the door to the left and were met by an old man in a black robe with wide, billowing sleeves. Seong Min paid for their lodgings for the night and ordered a meal to be prepared for them after they finished their baths. The old man then led them through a sliding door into the changing room. A row of wooden buckets, each with its own long-handled ladle protruding from it, sat in front of squat stools. Attendants filled the buckets with fresh water, and Yeong-Su and his brothers began to undress.

Yeong-Su took off his helmet and put it on a shelf. He then slid off his golden scale armor, stood it against the wall, and placed the heavy boots beside it. His shirt and pants had became sweat-soaked again, and he was happy to pull them off and give them to the attendants to be washed. As Yeong-Su sat in front of one of the buckets, he caught a glimpse of Ha Jun out of the corner of his eye and gasped.

His younger brother, Ha Jun, had also undressed. Yeong-Su's eyes roved up and down the sculpted body of muscle that was, even more incredibly, covered with scars. He had never seen so many long, dark marks crisscross someone's flesh.

"What happened to you?" Yeong-Su asked in amazement. He leaned closer, and Seong Min and Su Won turned towards Ha Jun. "Were you tortured in battle? But that can't be right, you couldn't have been a solider already. You're only sixteen."

Yeong-Su looked at Su Won and Seong Min for confirmation. Su Won stared in open curiosity, but conflicting emotions wrinkled Seong Min's face. Ha Jun directed his gaze to the ground, his naked body shaking as if he were cold.

"Yeong-Su," Seong Min said, "our time is short. Take your bath quickly so that we can eat." To the group, he said, "We have many hard days ahead of us, and this might be our last peaceful night to rest. Don't waste it."

Throughout the bath, Yeong-Su kept glancing at Ha Jun's body. There was a perceivable artistry to the injuries his younger brother had sustained. Whoever had wielded the whip had possessed a keen eye and a deft wrist.

When they finished, they went to the common room where men and women gathered together in loose robes. Seong Min had ordered samgyeopsal. The foreigner hadn't arrived, and it seemed like his brothers talked more freely and laughed more loudly without her there. Attendants had prepared their table with bowls of steaming rice, a basket of green lettuce leaves, salad, and small round saucers of onions, hot peppers, garlic, and kimchi. Green bottles of soju dotted the table. Ha Jun served soju to each of them in the tiny glasses, and then Seong Min took the bottle from him and poured a shot of the soju into Ha Jun's glass. When the thick slabs of pork were laid out over the charcoal on the metal grills, Seong Min stood and raised his glass.

"Younger brothers," he said, "I formally greet you as my companions. In the coming weeks, we will all have to inspire each other to keep ourselves strong when danger surrounds us and protect each other with the sword as well as the promise that we all make it back here to our families alive! You have met my wife and son. I have met your mentor and your parents."

Yeong-Su glanced at Ha Jun, who lowered his eyes.

"But now, and forever going forward, we are family. Our tales of heroism will be told to our children and our children's children. Our names will be praised, our deeds heralded. We leave now as regular men, but we will come back as heroes!"

Yeong-Su and Su Won erupted in cheer. Ha Jun made no sound, his glass raised before him, his hand shaking. Yeong-Su didn't know who his parents were, but he knew that one of their company would have to return back to the boy's mother or father to report their son's death. The boy wasn't ready for the quest they'd been given. Ak-ma were fearsome foes, attacking both the body and the spirit. Yeong-Su wondered why the governor had not reassigned or delayed Ha Jun when they discovered the true nature of the quest.

"Eat up tonight," Seong Min said, "and sleep well. I am sorry that we don't have time to get you women to keep you company."

Yeong-Su and Su Won cursed their fate even as they erupted in laughter.

"But when you return home, tales of your heroism will net you the most beautiful bride Jeju has to offer. Every girl will be eager to become your wife and bear your children."

Their curses turned to cheers. The four men drained their glasses of soju, the strong liquor burning its way down their throats and into their stomachs. Yeong-Su set down his cup as Ha Jun once again refilled their glasses. Yeong-Su chose the most tender cube of pork on the hot grill and placed it in the center of a leaf of lettuce. He dabbed gochu paste on the pork, then put rice and garlic on top and rolled it into a tight bundle.

"Older Brother," he said, leaning over to Seong Min, who opened his mouth so that Yeong-Su could pop the galbi in. He did this again for Su Won, and finally prepared the rolled pork combination for Ha Jun.

"Younger Brother." Yeong-Su bowed to Ha Jun. "Please accept my apology for earlier. I shouldn't have stared like that, and I am ashamed to have embarrassed you."

Ha Jun swallowed, his eyes cast downward. Quietly, he said, "I am not used to being around so many people. I spend most of my time alone with my father."

"Where are you from?"

"Hyuae."

Yeong-Su nodded, picturing the location in his head. The hallabang trees bore bright oranges, a specialty of Jeju Island, during the winter. The hallabang oranges were sold to wealthy officials across the mainland of Hanguk. Wrapped in colorful boxes, tied with red ribbons, and marked by the family's crest, the fruit tasted of spring days. Each orange slice burst in a person's mouth, making their lips tingle with the sweet and sour juice that dribbled down their chins.

"I know the area, and have passed it many times. Jeju's most famous oranges come from Hyuae. *Kang Hallabangs*."

Ha Jun's face flushed. "That is my father's farm. It's where I live."

Seong Min and Su Won overheard, and Seong Min asked, "Your father is Kang Jeong Seok?"

Ha Jun nodded, and the other three gasped in amazement.

"You are very fortunate," Yeong-Su said. "Kang Farms grow the most delicious oranges on Jeju. My father serves them when dignitaries from the mainland visit in the winter. They are so much more expensive on the mainland, and the guests are always impressed at how many we have available for them to eat."

Yeong-Su reached over and squeezed Ha Jun's arm, and noted that his muscles felt harder than stone. "Incredible," he breathed out, and wondered how powerful a blow his little brother could deliver. "Is that how you got so strong? Working on your father's farm?"

"I help my family every winter alongside the hired hands," he said, "but it's my father's special training that enabled me to become who I am today."

Yeong-Su wanted to ask about the scars crisscrossing Ha Jun's body, but Seong Min was staring at him. Instead, Yeong-Su motioned to Ha Jun with the rolled pork he still held. Ha Jun opened his mouth, and Yeong Su popped it in. Picking up the shot glass of soju, Yeong-Su stood and held it before him. "I am happy that you were selected to join us on this quest. To Ha Jun!"

"To Ha Jun!" Seong Min and Su Won shouted. The four of them clinked their glasses together, then downed the fiery liquor.

CHAPTER SEVEN

Captain Shiwoo stood in the center of the ferry's cargo hold. The cries of seagulls awakening on the wharf echoed against the wooden planks as the ship bobbed at the dock. They had not even set out on the Hanguk Strait yet, and already the waves had turned rough. A storm was brewing and approaching the island on violent winds.

Merchants had brought their cargo to the ferry throughout the night, and the crew had loaded them against the hulls, stacking the goods two and three crates high. The smell of salted black pork, Jeju's specialty, dried seafood, vegetables, and fruit filled the hull. The trip to Nokdong was their shortest route, taking only three hours. With the leeward wind, they'd get there quicker, so they carried more perishable goods since they could be unloaded and sent to open markets immediately.

The nineteen deckhands sat on the crates, long pipes between their lips. They all wore loose hemp clothes for quick movement in the hot summer weather. The helmsman, Tae Hyun, wore a hanbok with red swirls along the seams. Shiwoo also wore a hanbok, and a white hat with a wide white bill curling up in the front. On his waist were a curved dagger and a short sword.

"Last night," Shiwoo said above the sound of waves slapping against the hull, "that boy we brought back visited me in a dream. And he called forth all of those doomed boys we've carried across these waters, and they spat at my feet because I took coin to ferry them to their deaths."

Murmurs of distress rose from the deckhands. They spat on the deck to ward off angry souls left to wander the world in sorrow.

"That won't be enough," Shiwoo warned the sailors, his voice raspy from breathing in seawater every day of his life. "The dead of Jeju told me we have a duty to the people of island. A duty to their mothers and fathers, their sisters and brothers, their lovers and children left behind to grieve their lost. They said the dead have had enough, they said we can't let that foreigner take any more of our young men to the grave." He laid his hand on the hilt of his dagger. "They said that the foreigner must be stopped. She must die, and we're the only ones that can do it. That is our mission. That is our quest!"

The deckhands pulled short swords and daggers from their belts and raised them above their heads. "She can't take any more," they said. "She must go to the grave. That is our mission. That is our quest!"

Only the helmsman did not pull his weapons from his belt. He looked around at the deckhands waving their blades, worry creasing lines into his face.

"I will talk to the company coming on board today,"

Shiwoo continued. "I'll make them understand exactly what they're dealing with."

Shiwoo knew it wouldn't be hard to get at least one of the companions in a private conversation. The foreigner always sat apart from each new group, wrapped up in her own dark thoughts. Shiwoo had known of the woman for as long as he could remember. She hadn't aged even as he had grown from a child to a man.

Once, his father had operated the boat service, ferrying goods and passengers across the Hanguk Strait to the mainland. Shiwoo remembered the Dark Elf from even then, more than forty years ago. He'd grown from childhood to adulthood with her leading so many of the island men to their deaths. Of course, not all of the men died, but most of them definitely did not come back to Jeju alive. Yet he couldn't remember a time that the foreigner came back wounded. The cold look on her face never changed. Whether a hero returned to the island or just dead bodies, her expression remained the same.

When Shiwoo's father had submitted an application for his son to go on a quest, Shiwoo's fear had gotten the better of him, and he had refused to go. To this day, he remembered his father's disappointment, that gaze cutting him so deep that decades later he still bled on the inside. And it was all because of that soulless foreigner.

"The company of companions must listen to me," Shiwoo growled into the silence that had fallen over the deckhands as the past washed over him. "They must be warned about the danger. They must be made to realize their mission will fail if she's allowed to accompany them." Shiwoo clenched his left hand into a fist and raised his short sword over his head with his right. "Together, we'll gut her and hang her corpse from the leeboard for all to know, living and dead, that justice has finally been done."

The deckhands roared their approval, stomping their feet on the wooden planks of the hull and beating their hands on the crates. The worry lines in Tae Hyun's face deepened, and frustration welled up inside of Shiwoo. Why didn't his helmsman realize he was doing this for the good of humanity? That woman was something else, something unclean, something evil. Shiwoo had heard that one of the companions they were transporting to the quest today was only sixteen years old. Sixteen! That boy deserved to live, not get killed under the blue and brown gaze of that cursed woman.

"They'll be here soon," Shiwoo said as rays of light crept through the deck boards to penetrate the dim hold. "Send them down here and wait until I give the signal."

The deckhands cheered again, then scattered and climbed the ladders leading to the deck to prepare for the trip. Shiwoo waited for them all to leave until he was alone with his helmsman, who remained seated. He looked at Tae Hyun, who was six years older than he was.

"The dead visited you last night?" Tae Hyun asked quietly.

Shiwoo shrugged. "I see the dead in my dreams. They've visited me many nights."

"So today you will kill the foreigner? You're aware that she's under protection of the government?"

"But she's hated by the people of the island." Shiwoo paused, and allowed several breaths to pass before he casually asked, "You don't agree with my decision?"

"You're the captain," Tae Hyun replied without hesitation. "Your decision is yours to make. But the foreigners are mysterious, like the ocean deep. It may be foolish to dive into their depths without knowing what's waiting at the bottom in the dark."

Shiwoo barked out a harsh laugh. "It's a woman!" He slid the curved blade back into his belt. "A woman who carries no weapons. How will she be able to defend herself? How would she ever stop me?"

"So you would attack a defenseless woman?"

Shiwoo grew hot at the question. "There's something cursed about that foreigner," he said through clenched teeth. "She kills those boys somehow."

"Then we should discover proof of her crimes," Tae Hyun advised, "and present them to the governor. Let the law decide her fate."

"The bodies she brings back are the proof!" The words exploded from Shiwoo, his body shaking. "Proof enough for me. Yet still she's allowed to go and commit her crimes."

He leaned in close to Tae Hyun, who had still not risen from the crate.

"How do you explain each group of heavily armed men, Jeju's finest, going to the mainland and not coming back?" Shiwoo demanded of him. "Yet that foreigner, she goes and comes back without a scratch. Tell me, Tae Hyun, have you ever even seen her bleed?"

Tae Hyun glanced away, and Shiwoo laughed.

"It is strange," Tae Hyun admitted, "that in my forty-five years, I have never seen an injury on her. But the governors have been sending her off on quests for as long as anyone can remember. Even the current governor became a hero while in her company. When she tells the tales that we all remember, we know them to be true. A hundred years ago, she was there as men became heroes. A hundred years from now, she will be there as men become heroes. No one knows if the foreigners even die."

"And that's a comfort to you?" Shiwoo spun from Tae Hyun in disbelief. "The foreigners may not be able to die, and our leaders rise from those who come back from quests with them, and this doesn't worry you?" Shiwoo slapped a nearby crate. "Because it worries me! It keeps me up at night wondering if she's cast some kind of spell on the governors. Even upon the Emperors themselves, made heroes while watched over by those foreigners with their blue-brown eyes."

"Shiwoo," Tae Hyun gasped. "Careful of what you say!"

"No!" Shiwoo laid his hand on the hilt of his sword again. "I'm going to cut that woman open and see what her insides are made of. I'm going to slay the evil this time, and set the people of South Hanguk free."

CHAPTER EIGHT

Seong Min stirred first. He shook his younger brothers awake, and together, they went downstairs so as not to disturb the bathhouse's other guests. Through the windows, the light of dawn touched the sky. The sleepy sun rose from the sea and painted the clouds various hues of bright orange and yellow.

The old man in black robes greeted them, and directed the companions to a table laid out with fish, rice, kimchi, and soup. They dined, and then went back into the changing room to bathe and dress. Afterwards, they gathered their weapons and stepped outside into the brisk morning. Along the main lane leading to the governor's office, merchants set up their wares in front of shops. The high-pitched squeals of babies' wails drifted from nearby homes.

A buggy waited for them in front of the jjimjilbang, the driver and foreigner already on its perch. Seong Min wondered if she had slept well, and if she'd already eaten.

She didn't acknowledge them as they exited the bathhouse. Seong Min frowned. She didn't talk to the companions, but they also didn't speak to her. Perhaps they were all waiting for the other to make the first move; that waiting could last the entire journey.

Seong Min decided that he would try and hold a conversation with the foreigner later in the day. She may rebuff him at first, but he would remain persistent until the window of silence between them shattered.

He climbed into the freshly scrubbed wagon, and his brothers followed him. The driver snapped the reins, and the horses cantered down the city lane to the docks.

The acute aroma of fish and fresh water closed in upon them as they neared the docks. Seagulls circled above their heads. Their lulling cries rolled through the wharf. When the buggy stopped in front of the ferry, an oval shaped vessel with a reddish hull, Seong Min and his brothers climbed out and ascended the gangplank. The captain waited for them, his face twisted as if he'd recently eaten something rotten. When he noticed Seong Min watching him, he tried to relax his expression, but failed.

"Is there something wrong?" Seong Min asked him.

The captain stared at Seong Min for several seconds. "After we set off, I'd like to have a word with you in private."

His breath stank of alcohol and garlic, and the intensity in his eyes made Seong Min wary. Distrust blossomed in Seong Min's thoughts. With a frown, he nodded acceptance of the meeting. The ferry had been commissioned by the governor's office, after all, and perhaps the captain had a pressing matter to discuss with him. But the captain's eyes shone too brightly and shifted continuously from side to side as if some feverish secret brewed under his wide-brimmed hat, and he was desperately trying to keep his inner self under control. If there was betrayal in the works, no matter how unlikely that seemed, Seong Min had to be prepared for it.

The company passed the leering captain and embarked on the ferry. The foreigner trailed behind them. One of the deckhands led the way down a ladder into the cargo hold, and they chose the far end to sit together on crates of goods being shipped from Jeju to Nokdong.

"We're the only passengers?" Seong Min asked the longhaired deckhand.

The crewman took the pipe from his mouth, pursed his lips, and exhaled sweet-smelling smoke. "If the weather doesn't turn, we'll have more down here for the second trip of the day. But this early in the morning, you've got the hold to yourselves."

Seong Min realized that he and his brothers were outnumbered at least four to one. The sailors had knives and short swords tucked into their loose hemp clothes, and they moved with incredible agility aboard the bobbing ship. Their weapons would be ideal in these close quarters. Seong Min looked around and imagined him and his brothers wielding their longer swords in a crowded melee. They would never be able to maneuver around the hanging ropes in the narrow passageway. That disadvantage could prove fatal in an ambush.

Seong Min leaned his fire lance on the crates beside him. He would never use it on a wooden boat, as that would ensure no one would make it to shore. He placed his swords on his lap and instructed the others to do the same. Soon, the ferry drifted away from the dock, and the cries of seagulls grew faint. Su Won unwrapped dried squid and tore it into strips that he shared with the rest of them. Seong Min glanced at the foreigner, who sat several crates away from them. She certainly didn't encourage any conversational advances, her gaze perpetually unfocused as if deep in thought.

Seong Min sighed. Looking away from her, he noticed Ha Jun's broadsword. Its hilt was bronze, and ten intricate glyphs were inscribed in the thick metal.

"Younger brother," Seong Min said, curious, "may I hold your blade?"

Ha Jun stood and handed the sword to Seong Min with both hands. Seong Min took it, and doubled over as the heavy weapon brought him to the cargo hold's floor. Su Won and Yeong-Su inhaled sharply.

"How is this possible?" Seong Min tried to heave the weapon up. "It's like trying to rip a tree out by the roots."

Only by crouching and using his legs was he able to pry the sword up from the wooden planks of the hold's floor. Seong Min could barely stand up straight, and he was forced to keep the blade on his shoulder, his arms not strong enough to wield it.

"Is it really that heavy, Older Brother?" Yeong-Su asked.

"You want to try it?" Seong Min motioned to his younger brother. He handed it to him and laughed as Yeong-Su dropped to the hull just as he had.

"What kind of weapon is this?" Seong Min asked as Su Won went to help Yeong-Su lift the blade. Only together were they able to get it off the floor.

"It's a glyph sword," Ha Jun answered. "There's magic in it."

Seong Min noticed that the foreigner followed their conversation, her head inclined in their direction.

"How does it work?" Yeong-Su asked.

"I'm not entirely sure," Ha Jun admitted. "I've had it all my life. This sword is my first memory."

He slid the blade out of its sheath, and the glyphs, inscribed there, too, were etched along the metal. "These represent strength and speed. Whoever crafted the weapon made it unnaturally heavy, and the only way to master it is to start wielding it from early childhood."

Ha Jun spun the sword deftly in his palm, and Seong Min, Yeong-Su, and Su Won leaned back in awe.

"I started trying to lift it not long after I learned to walk. I remember the first time I got it a couple of centimeters off the floor. I was about seven years old." Ha Jun spun the weapon again, and it whistled through the air. "When I was ten, I carried it around with me everywhere I went. When I helped my father on the farm, or my uncle on his ranch." Ha Jun paused, his face darkening. "I would always wear it on my back," he continued after a moment. "It feels like a part of me now." He slid the sword back into its sheath, sat down on a crate, and rested it on his lap.

Seong Min exchanged glances with Yeong-Su and Su Won. Magic weapons were rare and expensive, and there was a certain foreignness to those glyphs that couldn't be ignored. He was careful not to look at the foreigner, but he had a feeling that her kind had a hand in crafting the weapon. Elven-made magical weapons were as powerful as they were expensive. How Ha Jun's family had gotten hold of one, and how much they had paid for it, was definitely to be considered later. It had to be no less than a fortune. With a financial sacrifice like that, what had they done to ensure that Ha Jun wouldn't disappoint them? Since debt passed from father to son, Ha Jun's children's children's children could one day be paying for the blade.

The deckhand from earlier stuck his head down into the hold from the top of the ladder. "Captain wants to have a word with you," he said to Seong Min. "We're halfway to Nokdong."

Seong Min nodded, and to his younger brothers, said, "I'll be back in a moment."

He left his fire lance propped against the crates, but he took his sword, strapped it to his waist, and climbed up the ladder to the deck. A strong wind buffeted him as he came up out of the hold, and the spray from the Hanguk Strait made the wooden planks slippery. Dark clouds hovered above them, and the wind whipped the ferry through the churned up high waves that crashed against the hull. Ahead, the coast drew near at a fast clip. They would be docking soon, and he wondered what the captain wanted to speak to him about.

Seong Min stumbled after the deckhand to the deckhouse, where the captain sat on one of many barrels lining the wide room. The barrels were tied by thick rope attached to the hull so that they would not topple over. Half a dozen hammocks swung from the ceiling, and various swords, daggers, and axes were secured to the hull around the room. The captain had placed a long dark bottle and two glasses on one of the barrels, and he motioned for Seong Min to sit down next to him.

"Sake from Il-Bon Nala." He poured clear liquor into the two glasses and handed one to Seong Min. "Thank you for joining me."

"Thank you for inviting me," Seong Min said out of politeness. They clinked glasses and sipped the sake. It tasted of lightly flavored water, and it slid smoothly down his throat, quenching his thirst.

The captain studied him closely. Seong Min, swishing the liquor in his mouth, swallowed and said, "It's delicious."

The captain nodded. "And very rare. A friend ships them to wealthy families on the mainland. Sometimes he'll have a few extra bottles, which he sells to sailors working at the docks. The ones that can afford it normal price, that is."

The two men drained their glasses, and the captain refilled Seong Min's sake. "How old are you?" he asked.

"Twenty-six."

"Married?"

Seong Min nodded. "I have a son. Almost two years old now."

The captain's smile revealed several gold teeth. "There's nothing more fortunate than sons," he said. Seong Min nodded in agreement.

"Where's your hometown?"

"Seongsan," Seong Min replied. "My family runs a restaurant and boarding house there."

"I know the area well. I've hiked Ilchulbong Sunrise Peak with my family. My wife and daughters live in Hamdeok." He frowned. "All girls so far. I'm not as fortunate as you. I've gotten old, but my wife is ten years younger. We'll try again, and hopefully this time we'll be granted a son."

"I wish you luck." Seong Min raised his glass, and the two men drank the sake again.

The captain stared at Seong Min in silence, and Seong Min was unsure how the conversation should continue. The meeting wasn't going as he had envisioned it. That devious look the captain had worn when they boarded the ship had been replaced with concern. Even worry. Something was definitely wrong, but Seong Min couldn't guess what it could be.

"I've been taking men, most as old as you, some younger, to the mainland for years. Married men, engaged men, men with mothers who shed tears as they left on the quests, men whose fathers wished them a successful journey and speedy return. And I have brought back many bodies. Too many bodies, torn apart sometimes, drenched with blood. Dead. Dead. Dead!"

The captain stared out the door at the deck. "I don't want to bring back your corpses across these waters. I don't want to see your wife weeping, and your son crying for a father that's never going to wake up again."

"We won't fail," Seong Min said, touched by the captain's words. "Please don't worry about us. My brothers are strong, and we will succeed at our quest."

"I know you'll give it your all," the captain said, "and I want to do what I can to make sure nothing stops you before you've even gotten your chance." The captain leaned towards Seong Min and lowered his voice. "That foreign woman. She must die!"

Seong Min jerked back from the captain, who darted closer like a snake.

"Is this a joke?" Seong Min asked, though the feral look that swept the captain's face answered the question.

"She kills them," he growled, and Seong Min's fingers itched to grasp the hilt of his sword. "She goes off with the boys, they come back in pieces, and she comes back whole. I tell you, she kills them."

Seong Min couldn't back any farther from the captain without standing, but something told him that the man might overreact to the gesture. He tried to reason with him instead.

"We can't kill her." He frowned as if weighing the option. "She's protected by the governor."

The captain flapped his hand in front of Seong Min's face as if waving a foul odor away. "That's their evil plot at work. She must kill the ones who she can't control and let those who fall under her spell take the highest levels of power. The mayors, the governors." The captain's eyes shined. "Even the Emperor," he whispered.

Seong Min needed to escape the cabin, but that wouldn't resolve the situation. "I can't help you do this." He kept his voice steady even as his thoughts drifted to the dire reality of the situation. Would he really fight humans to save an elf? Would he really kill his own people to save a foreigner? No, but somehow, he had to convince the captain that this plot was madness.

"You don't have to bloody your hands." The captain's gold teeth twinkled as his smile widened further. "I'll take pleasure in doing it on my own. I've seen what she's done to our people. I know the horror of their torn apart bodies. I'll gut that woman for us, to avenge our country of her foul deeds."

At this, Seong Min stood, and the captain shot to his

feet also. "Let me think on it," Seong Min said, backing away from that feverish gaze.

"There's no time. We should be pulling up to the docks any moment now. You don't have to do anything, just lead your companions off the ship. She'll come out last, she always does. And we'll be there waiting for her."

CHAPTER NINE

Raindrops dripped through the deck boards into the hold and pattered on Ha Jun and his brothers. He felt the ferry's direction change. The slap of the deckhands' swift feet resounded above him as they lowered the sail.

"They're slowing us down," Su Won said. "The current's too strong today."

The waves slapped against the hull, and a shrill wind whipped past the ferry. Seagulls' cries once again punctuated the air. As the ferry slowed, its bobbing motion became more pronounced, the waves carrying the boat up higher and dropping it down faster. A deckhand descended the ladder into the hold, followed by Seong Min, who was in turn followed by two more deckhands. The meeting between his older brother and the captain had lasted a long time. Ha Jun thought the expression on Seong Min's face seemed tight.

Su Won approached Seong Min. "Older Brother? Has something happened?"

The deckhands stood on either side of Seong Min. "The Strait's rough today, but we'll be docking soon," he said. "Collect your things and be ready to disembark."

Seong Min slung his fire lance around his shoulder. Ha Jun grabbed his pouch and slipped his sword into his hanbok at the waist. They waited as the captain issued commands to the ferry's crew, and at a sudden bump against the hull, the deckhands in the hold pointed up the ladder.

"We're docked," one said.

Seong Min went up first, followed by Yeong-Su and Su Won. After Ha Jun, the three deckhands came. Windshine climbed up onto the deck last. The rest of the crew gathered loosely near the lowered gangplank. Ha Jun wondered when they would start to unload the merchandise, which seemed like a difficult job by the number of crates tied down below. Seong Min, Yeong-Su, and Su Won walked down the gangway towards the docks. Ha Jun started down and looked over his shoulder to see how far Windshine was trailing behind. He had become accustomed to this habit of hers and had been wondering how he could break her of it.

The deckhands suddenly closed in behind him and drew their short swords. Ha Jun spun around, surprised, and Yeong-Su ran back up the gangplank, his heavy boots thudding on the wooden board.

"What's going on here?" Ha Jun demanded of them. "What do you think you're doing?"

Ha Jun looked past the deckhands and saw that the captain had cornered Windshine near the railing, his sword pointed at her.

"You don't have to take any action, son." The

helmsman stood with the deckhands. "The captain is doing this for you."

Yeong-Su stood beside Ha Jun. "Has he lost his mind?" the mayor's son asked. "The Dark Elf is a governor's aide. She's appointed by the Emperor. She can't be harmed."

The captain was spitting words at Windshine so fast and with such crazed vehemence that Ha Jun couldn't grasp the meaning of the man's diatribe. Something about spirits, and death, and schemes to destroy South Hanguk. The Dark Elf didn't seem to be responding, her features impassive, her hands by her sides despite the blade trained upon her.

"She has no weapon," Ha Jun cried out. He turned to Seong Min, who stood behind him on the gangplank. "We have to help her."

Yeong-Su turned to Seong Min also. "We can't stand by while she's attacked. She's protected by the highest laws of the country. We'd be complicit in her murder."

Seong Min's hands opened and closed before him. None of them had drawn their weapons. Though the deckhands held their short swords directed at them, it didn't seem that they harbored intent to use them against the brothers.

"Will we fight our countrymen?" Seong Min asked Yeong-Su. "Will we kill our own?"

Yeong-Su looked back at the deckhands and the helmsman. Ha Jun saw the captain suddenly swipe at Windshine, and his heart sped up. The Dark Elf dodged the blade, but the captain slid a curved dagger from his belt and sliced upwards, catching Windshine in the arm.

An arc of blood followed the dagger's trajectory and splattered on the deck boards.

The Dark Elf bled red, just like any human.

Ha Jun's heart beat so hard in his chest that he gasped. He pushed past Yeong-Su and Seong Min and sprinted down the wet gangway to the dock. Then he spun around, raced back up the gangplank, and jumped through the raindrops falling from the gray clouds above. He soared over the heads of the deckhands, who looked up at the height he'd gained in open-mouth amazement. He slammed into the mast, grabbed hold of the wooden pillar, and swung around so that he dropped to the deck next to Windshine.

"Ha Jun!" Seong Min called from the gangplank and cursed.

The captain's eyes opened wide at Ha Jun's sudden appearance.

"How?" he sputtered, backing away from Windshine.

Ha Jun immediately stepped in the space between them.

"Out of the way, boy," the captain snarled as realization dawned in his face. "Let me finish what I started."

"No!" The word, pushed forward by his racing heart, erupted from Ha Jun. His body pulsated, the ball of emotions buried inside of him awakening.

"Fool!" The captain slid the bloody dagger into his hanbok and reached out to grab Ha Jun.

Ha Jun caught his hand and twisted. There was a harsh cracking sound, followed by a long wail of pain. The deckhands turned to Ha Jun as the captain doubled over. The helmsman rushed towards them. He shouted commands at Ha Jun, but the drumming of Ha Jun's heart flooded his ears so much that the words were drowned by the wild beat. He closed his fingers on the captain's hand, and he felt the bones give in, snapping until the hand was pulp in his palm. The captain's screams tore from his mouth, his head bent over as he fell to his knees. Ha Jun reached forward to wrap his other hand around the captain's throat. The helmsman pulled his short sword from his hanbok. Ha Jun was faster, and just as his grip tightened around the captain's throat, something gentle touched his arm.

Ha Jun froze. A tempest roared in his mind, and he struggled to peer past it. He turned, slowly, to gaze into Windshine's blue-brown eyes. Her light touch upon his forearm reminded him of the peace that had descended upon him the first time he saw her.

Ha Jun's brothers broke through the deckhands' barrier and stood next to him. They still had not raised their weapons, but they remained firm in front of the blades pointed at them.

"You are not our enemies," Seong Min told them. "Let us go in peace."

The deckhands exchanged glances but didn't move. The rain fell harder. The wind whipped in from the Hanguk Strait and tore at their clothes, yet no one shifted from their positions.

Finally, the helmsman stepped forward. He stared at Windshine first, then Ha Jun. For several silent moments, he stared at the way Windshine touched Ha Jun. Conflicted emotions ran across his face, his short sword loosely held in his grasp. Then he sighed, long and low, as his shoulders drooped. The helmsman sheathed his weapon.

"The captain," he said to Ha Jun. "Please release him."

Ha Jun let go of the sobbing man. The captain dropped to his side, shuddered, and clutched his broken hand against his chest. The helmsman crouched beside him, but his eyes remained fastened on Windshine's touch on Ha Jun's arm.

"Go on, then." He nodded towards the docks. "You're free to do as you please."

CHAPTER TEN

Windshine pressed her hand against the cut on her arm. The blade hadn't slashed her too deep, but the wound bled through her fingers. Ha Jun walked beside her, the first time he'd done so since they'd met. The vibrating sphere of condensed energy alive inside of him appeared as a tight ball of highly charged emotion in her vision. All that power inside of a human! He reminded her of an elf, and she longed to connect with him and experience something familiar in this foreign land.

Su Won came to her side. "I can help you," he said.

These were the first words he had spoken to her since they'd met. He was the stoutest of the men, and had a shaved head glistening in the rain. For a human, his eyes were wise, as if he'd seen mysteries as great as they were rare. Many of the monks in South Hanguk had similar profound expressions. For this reason, Windshine avoided them whenever possible, believing it would be a mistake to give them the chance to discern too many of her true thoughts.

She could heal her own wound, but all four of the companions watched her, and she didn't want to bring greater suspicion upon herself. Restraining her true abilities while trying to figure out a way to escape the captain without injuring any of the humans had left her exposed and allowed him to wound her. The trickle of blood snaking down her arm made her head light, as if it would float from her shoulders at any moment. She had planned to wait until the companions slept to take care of it. Now that the monk offered his services, Windshine decided it might be best to let him take care of it now.

Holding out her arm, Windshine silently watched as Su Won gripped her bicep. He held the golden three-legged medallion in his other hand. He chanted words in a Hangugeo dialect that fluttered around her but refused to be understood. Not grasping the chants made her suspicious. Too much power existed between the intones. After all of these centuries, she often forgot that humans could still do things she didn't quite understand and so may not be able to successfully counter.

Her muscle involuntarily tightened as warmth spread through her. The skin around the cut curled in upon itself and closed. The blood stopped, but her flesh still stung.

The captain's dagger had also ripped through her tunic. The monk could do nothing about that. She would have to mend the cloth later while the humans slept.

"Thank you," Windshine said to Su Won.

His round face flushed, and he mumbled something that she could not catch before he rejoined the others walking several steps ahead.

Nokdong was a small village surrounded by rice paddies. The small gray stone houses with thatched roofs stood far apart from each other, separated by green fields and farms. When the companions had traveled far and the ocean's salty smell had faded, Seong Min turned to the group.

"The official on Jeju said there's a ranch here that rents out horses. It shouldn't be much farther away."

They followed him down narrow dirt lanes winding across fields and through trees. As the morning wore on, the humidity increased even as the rain persisted. Eventually, Seong Min stopped at a house to ask for directions. The man who answered the door, his three children gathered behind him and staring curiously at the armed company, said, "You're off to Suncheon?"

Seong Min nodded.

"You're not the first." He looked at Windshine. "Others are on the same quest. You'll have to travel fast if you want to catch them." He pointed north. "The ranch is that way."

Seong Min thanked him, and as they walked away, the man said, "There're rumors that only fools are challenging the ak-ma. Fools soon to be dead men."

They followed the path with his words lingering in their thoughts. The fresh smell of dung announced that they reached the ranch. A large field came into view where a dozen horses wandered around a long barn with a wooden steeple roof. A rancher wearing a long-sleeved white shirt and a yellow vest threw hay into a trough. He looked up as the companions approached, and under the wide brim of his bamboo hat, his eyes narrowed upon seeing Windshine.

"Greetings, sir." Seong Min bowed. "I am Seong Min, and these are my younger brothers. We are from the island of Jeju on our way to Suncheon and were told we could rent horses here. Is that possible?"

The rancher removed a pipe from the pocket of his loose purple pants and lit it. "Buy," he said after a puff. "You can buy five of my horses."

"I'm sorry, sir, perhaps we've been steered wrong." Seong Min bowed in apology. "We're only here to rent horses, not buy. Is there another rancher in this area?"

"There isn't, and you weren't steered wrong." He focused on Windshine again. "I don't rent horses to men in the company of their kind. South Hanguk people don't come back often when involved with those foreigners."

The four men glanced at Windshine, but she remained silent.

Seong Min clasped his hands together. "It would make our journey so much easier if we were to ride," he implored the rancher. "Please, sir, are you sure we can't come to an arrangement?"

The rancher puffed on his pipe. "You can arrange to buy them," he replied. "My horses aren't to rent if you ride out with her."

Seong Min couldn't move the rancher to change his mind, so the companions left the ranch. The steady rain soured their moods further, their hanboks clinging to them like second skins. Away from the Strait, the wind didn't blow. The summer's humidity gathered close around them and made the air oppressive. Windshine noticed that Ha Jun continued to walk by her side. She slowed her pace so that he would catch up with the other men, but he slowed down with her. Despite the dreary situation, Windshine buried a smile at this child beside her. What would he think if he knew she neared a thousand years old?

His power, that bright star tethered inside of him, reminded her of male Dark Elves. For a human, he had handsome features. His cheekbones were well defined, his eyes sharp with curiosity and burning with life. But he was only sixteen, and he was at that human age where his attention to her could intensify to blind attraction in an instant. Windshine didn't need some human man tripping over himself in her presence, especially on the dangerous road they'd be traveling. Ha Jun needed to remain sharp so he could be there for his human companions. She slowed to a snail's pace until the other three were far ahead. When he did the same, she couldn't bear to reprimand him.

Seong Min turned to them, and when he saw how far they had fallen behind the group, he called to Ha Jun to catch up. The boy hesitated with a sideways glance at Windshine, but Seong Min called him again. He had no choice but to jog forward to catch up with his companions.

They walked along a mud path leading out of Nokdong. Windshine had both walked and ridden through all of South Hanguk. She knew well the rancher that had refused them the horses she knew well. As a child, he used to stare at her with curiosity, gentle and pure as only an inquisitive human in their beginning years managed to do. She remembered the man's father, and his father's father, going back generations. The rancher had grown into an old man, the kindness replaced by bitter mistrust. She had said nothing as he refused to rent them horses, but she still saw him as a child in the fields beyond that same house, running around with his siblings and laughing at the silly things kids amused themselves with to keep boredom at bay.

Because of her, Seong Min seemed to have decided that they would walk to Suncheon. The journey would take two days at least, putting them behind schedule. If the rain became a storm, that could slow down their speed to three days. Seong Min probably would blame her for the fact that they couldn't get there faster on horseback as he had planned. He wouldn't be happy with her at this delay, not to mention the fact that Ha Jun, even now, kept glancing back at her. Before the day ended, she wondered if Seong Min would regret that the captain hadn't had the opportunity to finish her on the boat, removing her as a burden to their quest.

At a break in the rainfall several hours later, Seong Min led them to a short stone wall built around a rice patty, and they sat down for lunch. Windshine settled away from them and took out dried strips of pork and a mound of rice. She bit into the salty meat, placed some rice into her mouth with the tips of her fingers, and chewed. She heard footsteps, and looked up to see Seong Min and Su Won approached her. She tensed, and quickly checked to see if they had unsheathed their swords.

Without a word, Su Won picked up her pork and rice, and Seong Min took her hand.

"That's enough of that, Older Sister." Seong pulled her to her feet. He led her to where they sat, his fingers wrapped around hers. "Please sit down and join us for lunch."

Her breath caught in her throat. For a moment, Windshine silently beheld the men challenging the solitude she'd known for centuries. No group of companions she'd traveled with had been as strange and behaved as unexpectedly as this group. She could return back to the spot they took her from, but Su Won held her food, and she didn't have enough provisions to waste any. Plus, the way Seong Min stared at her made her realize that he would just repeat his action and bring her back over to them. These companions and their stubborn ways shook her grasp of reality. Windshine kept a smile at bay and sat beside the companions.

"You lost a lot of blood today," Su Won said. "You need to eat more than this." He handed her pork and rice back, then added kettle fish, dried anchovies, kimchi, an additional helping of rice and pork, and poured cold seaweed soup from a wide flask into a small wooden cup. Windshine stared at the abundance of food, and realized she had more than the rest of them. She began to protest, but again, the look in their eyes made her realize it would be pointless.

"Thank you," she said.

They waited until she began to eat to continue with their meals. They didn't speak while a light drizzle started again. Yeong-Su, in his golden scale armor, offered a curse to the sky. Perhaps it decided to take pity upon them, for the rain didn't last long.

After they finished, the men took out pipes and lit them. Seong Min took a puff from his, then handed it to Windshine. She placed the wooden tip to her mouth and inhaled the sweet smoke. A pleasurable haze suffused her, her concerns loosening their grasp and easing her anxiety. She watched dragonflies with wings like vibrating rainbows chase gnats and mosquitoes that had been harassing the companions since they started their journey from the Strait. A thought had seeded itself in her desire to give something of importance back to this unusual group of brothers, and it relentlessly nagged at her. *It's a mistake,* she told herself, *you shouldn't do this*. But when she handed the pipe back to Seong Min, and the five of them remained seated there together in quiet contemplation, Windshine motioned to Ha Jun's sword.

"May I see that?" she asked.

Ha Jun hesitated a moment, then held the glyph sword outstretched to her.

"It's very heavy." He looked at her slender arms. "You might hurt yourself."

Windshine said nothing, and Ha Jun handed her the weapon. She flipped it over in her hand and released the blade from its sheath in a fluid, deft motion. The men sat upright and gasped in astonishment. She twirled the sword in her hand, then held it up and studied the blade.

"How are you doing that?" Seong Min asked in breathy awe. "We could barely lift it."

"I can do this," she replied, "because I'm the one who made it. Long before any of you were born." She swung the sword, and the blade whistled through the air.

Ha Jun had surprised her on the ferry with the ease with which he'd carried the weapon. When Windshine had crafted the sword decades ago, she had added a spell to make it too heavy for any human to easily use. It would take years of practice to wield the sword, and she figured most humans wouldn't have the patience, or the time, to master swinging the blade. But Ha Jun's father, the crafty human, had given the boy the weapon at a very young age. Children have the capacity to learn faster than adults because they're more open to possibilities. It never occurred to seven-year-old Ha Jun that it should be impossible for a boy his age to lift the sword.

Again, the voice in her head rose and warned her not to share the sword's secrets, that it would be a mistake to teach them the ways of Dark Elves. *You're not one of them, and the humans can't handle true power. Not even all Dark Elves could handle true power.*

Windshine had set off with twenty-five of her faction from their war-torn country when she was a young adult. Six hundred years old, Windshine had had to take care of her younger sister, Blythe, still a child at two hundred years old. Their mother had recently been killed by another faction, and their father sent them away to find new lives in a different world.

The elves' magic was vast, their weapons crafted for the specific purpose of destruction on massive scales. Their war had lasted so long because elves had extended lifespans. Her kind could exist thousands of years, and they remembered past injustices a millennium later as clearly as the first day. Every faction had a score to settle against a different faction, and no one wanted to let the sacrifices of their fallen comrades be in vain.

Century after century the elves fought. One clan would gain an upper hand over another and subjugate them to their will. It never lasted, as the conquered and the conqueror remained in constant flux. Finally, the elves came to a dark realization. One group would have to eliminate all the other groups if there would ever be peace. A single faction must arise and leave no hint of any other faction that could ever oppose them.

Genocide was the only way out of the thousands of years of war, and the elves all knew the evil that would have to be employed to make this a reality. Windshine's father, not wanting his daughters to be part of either the losing clan or, even worse, the ultimate winning clan, sent them away so that they could maintain their innocence. They sailed across the seas with a likeminded group who realized that the faction that eventually won would also eventually lose, their capacity to do good, to love, forever lost to them by the atrocities of their actions.

Before she left her country, Windshine and the other twenty-five had learned many of the magics of their homeland. She held Ha Jun's glyph sword before her and noted the perfections that she had crafted into the weapon. It was only one Elven item, she rationalized, and this company of humans was trying so hard to accept her as one of them. The loneliness she had kept at bay for years closed in upon her like a fist and threatened to strangle her.

When the Dark Elves had first arrived in South Hanguk, the Emperor from that era had given them asylum for fear that they would go to a neighboring country and be put to service there. But he had made them pay the price of solitude, as he forbid their kind to gather in groups larger than two. And he kept the same gender together so their number would remain the same as when they first arrived on South Hanguk's shores.

Windshine spun the sword in her hand again as the voice continued to plead with her, but it had been so long since she'd had a conversation.

"You're wrong about these." She indicated the inscriptions on the hilt and blade. "They aren't simply glyphs. They're spells written in my native tongue. This," she pointed out the first one, "is Elvish for earth. This is fire, and then water, wind, and electricity. There are five words on the hilt, and they repeat twice each on the blade."

Windshine stepped away from the companions. "To truly master the sword, you have to speak my language."

She raised the sword over her head, said, *"Earth!"*, in Elvish, and swung the blade down. It slammed into the muddy path and caused the land beneath their feet to rumble. The men leapt up and tried to maintain their footing as an earthquake roiled the farms. A chasm, meters thick, split open at Windshine's feet and stretched far out ahead of her.

She turned to the humans, who gaped in stupid astonishment.

"As you see," she said, allowing them to inspect the sword, "the inscription on the blade disappears when used. It takes about two or three days for the word to come back, depending on how much energy is expanded and how strong the spirit of the user who conjures the power is. Right now, I'm holding back," she admitted, "since this is just a demonstration. Watch."

She turned back to the chasm, said, *"Water!"*

She slashed the sword downwards in a sharp motion. A wave of water exploded from the blade and slammed into the earth, splintering the ground and filling the massive hole with clear liquid.

"Only the truly gifted can ever master the sword properly," Windshine said.

She swept the sword through the water and said, *"Electricity!"*

An electric current ripped through the liquid, and in a thunderclap, the chasm exploded. The shock wave lifted them off their feet and hurled them back over the wall into the rice paddy behind them. Windshine landed alongside the companions with a splash, the muddy water soaking her blue tunic. It took her a moment to stand, and when she did, her face flushed at the sight of the four companions who also struggled to their feet. They stared at her in silence for several moments before Seong Min spoke.

"The truly gifted, huh?"

This time, Windshine couldn't prevent the smile that budded on her face. It was mirrored by the four companions, and the smiles turned to quiet laughter as the muddy water dripped from their clothes.

CHAPTER ELEVEN

The rain let up as they travelled to Suncheon, even as the humidity worsened. Puddles lined the road and bred insects. Tiger mosquitoes buzzed in the companions' ears, snuck beneath their clothes, and left behind painful red bumps with an itch that burned with relentless vengeance. This led the group to frequent scratching beneath their hanboks. The companions paused so that Su Won could mix a salve made from lemon oil and eucalyptus. He spread it over their skin, but the relief didn't last long as their sweat from the intense humidity diluted the potion.

When Su Won wasn't mixing a new batch of the potion, he positioned himself beside Windshine and Ha Jun as the Dark Elf taught his younger brother the Elvish words to activate the magic in the sword. Humans never saw the elves write anything down, so Su Won was surprised when Windshine revealed that the glyphs on the sword belonged to the Elvish language. He wondered how many other items the elves had passed on to humans had

Elvish inscribed on them. What other magic lurked at the fingertips of the people of South Hanguk that they weren't aware of? Why did the Dark Elves not inform the humans of the hidden spells at work on the items given to man?

Su Won would have to tell the Order of the Monks and let his elders decide if they should relay the revelation to the government officials, for keeping this secret might be to the monks' future advantage.

For three days the companions walked the muddy road leading to Suncheon. At night, they gathered leaves to sleep on to avoid the wet ground. After a while, the farms along the road gave way to orchards. Just as Jeju was famous for its oranges, Suncheon was known for its large red and green apples.

"Look!" Su Won pointed. Large masses of brownish webbing covered the trees. An infestation of tent caterpillars had grown over all the orchards.

Seong Min asked, "Where are the farmers? And for that matter, where are other travelers to Suncheon?"

Su Won took hold of his golden three-legged crow pendant and extended his spiritual energy into the world around him. He sensed animal life, but no human life nearby.

"Something terrible has happened," Su Won said. "We should stop and see what it is."

Seong Min agreed. They took the next narrow path, turned off the road, and cut through an orchard. Moths fluttered around them in thick clouds, their wings brushing against their faces as they settled in their hair. The webbing in the trees obscured the leaves and created darkness under the boughs by blocking what little light fell from the cloudy sky.

"I wonder how long this has afflicted the land?" Su Won walked up to one of the trees and laid his hand against the bark. "Harvest begins next month."

"Not for these orchards," Seong Min said. "Nothing is going to grow here. There will be no income for these farmers this season."

The path led them to a small stone house with a thatched roof. The companions walked with heavy footsteps and spoke loudly as they approached it, not wanting to startle the farmer or family who lived there. Silence responded to their efforts. A sense of tragedy pervaded the area.

At the door, Seong Min knocked.

"Hello?" he called out. "We are travelers from Jeju. We're seeking information about the blight in the trees."

No answer. After several moments, Seong Min pushed the door open and stepped in. Even from outside, the rest of the companions saw it. Blood. It had been spattered on the walls, and stained the floor. Flies buzzed in the air, but a stench of death did not hover in the house because there no flesh to lay there and rot away in the humid air.

Seong Min turned to those standing outside.

"There's so much blood," he said, his face grim, "as if it'd been spilled out from basins. But there are no bodies. No corpses. Just blood, and it looks like enough to have flowed from several people."

Su Won stepped into the house beside Seong Min. He again took hold of the golden three-legged crow medallion with one hand, and touched the blood splattered against the wall with the other. He closed his eyes so that he could envision the barrier between the living world and the dead realm. The separation came into focus, a hazy veil that existed everywhere in both planes of existence. Through the touch of the blood, he sought out the spirits that had once occupied the bodies, but they did not dwell in the other realm. Instead, they shrieked in torment in a nearby place. Men, women, and children cried out in a cacophony of voices begging for release from some prison that held them.

Su Won braced himself and kept imploding his sense of reality until he reached the core of his inner self. He inspected this foundation from which everything that made him flowed, and he concentrated upon how his spirit fit perfectly within the casing of his flesh. Slowly, he vibrated his core, then faster, until the motion was so disruptive that Su Won managed to dislodge his soul.

Freed from the shell of his mortal form, he turned to the screams and followed them across the ether. He floated out of the stone farmhouse and drifted past his brothers and older sister, passing the dying trees. He followed the threads of horror connected to the blood. Soaring right below the heavy gray clouds, he flew down the muddy road until he saw Suncheon city. Farther still he went until he glimpsed the companion's destination: Jukdobong Forest. He noticed the trees moved without wind, but an unnatural fog obscured his spiritual vision and he could not discern how. Beyond Jukdobong Forest stood three mountains surrounding Naganeupseong Fortress. There Su Won flew towards. In the fortress settlement, he saw gray-skinned humans with bright green eyes. They wore colorless hanboks and carried swords on their hips. The tormented screams came from inside these armed hollow men.

Su Won drifted closer to get a better look, then

paused. The ethereal world darkened. He turned to the fortress, aware that a presence focused on him.

The presence approached, and Su Won backed away. Cold hatred emanated from the entity. Suddenly it grew a mouth full of fangs that opened wide and lunged at Su Won to consume him whole.

In a flash, Su Won's soul flung itself back into his body. He staggered and fell to his knees on the blood-stained floor, his breath coming out in harsh gasps.

"What is it?" Seong Min dropped down to help Su Won to his feet. "What did you see, Little Brother?"

The world spun around Su Won, and he closed his eyes as his stomach lurched. He wanted to run, to escape the image of the gray-faced humans with bright green eyes being controlled by that terrible entity in the fortress.

"They've been made into hollow men," Su Won said, his throat dry, his heart racing. "And they're waiting for us. All of us."

"We should get outside." Seong Min helped Su Won to his feet and led him back through the door.

Seong Min sat Su Won down in the grass and gave him seaweed soup in a wooden cup from their dwindling provisions. They waited as his breathing slowed and his hands stopped trembling so that he could answer their questions.

"What do you mean, they're hollow men?" Seong Min asked.

Su Won remained silent for a moment as he struggled to explain what he had witnessed. "They look like humans. They have gray skin and bright green eyes. But the souls inside of them belong to others, the families of this land. It's like the gray men are empty, and the South Hanguk people are trapped inside."

"How did it happen?"

"I'm not sure." Su Won shuddered. "Something's taken over the fortress."

"The ak-ma?"

Su Won nodded. "I was chosen for this mission because physical weapons won't stop the demon, but the Order of the Monks has an affinity for battling them. This ak-ma is malevolent, more so than I would have ever imagined. The farmers of the region were trying to cure the blight and meddled with spiritual forces they did not understand. Instead of helpful nature spirits, the ak-ma rose up. Its hatred is cold, and old. It wants to consume the country and turn us all into hollow men."

Su Won dropped his head, his next words heavy with doubt. "I will be honest. Even with my spiritual reservoir gathered from years of meditation, I don't know if I can beat the thing in the fortress on my own."

Seong Min put his hand on Su Won's shoulder. "You're not on your own," he said. "You've got your brothers to help you fight." He turned to the group. "But it is not in our favor that the ak-ma knows we're on our way. And it's taken up residence in Naganeupseong Fortress. On three sides, the fortress is surrounded by mountains. That makes approaching invaders easy to see. The only other way there is through Jukdobong Forest where sentries may be lying in wait. The ak-ma will see us before we see it, and it'll be prepared for our arrival."

Windshine stepped forward. "As you all must know, it is forbidden for me to help you complete your quest."

"Nor would we want it," Seong Min said, to which

Yeong-Su, Su Won, and Ha Jun agreed. "This is our country and our fight. It is up to us to take care of our own battles."

Windshine smiled. "But I can point something out. Ha Jun has learned the words of my language to use the spells inscribed on the sword. It will take time before he's able to maximize their power, but right now, he is formidable in wielding the weapon." To Su Won, she asked, "How many hollow men did you see?"

"Maybe a couple dozen," he said, "but there could have been more in the barracks surrounding the fortress."

"Even if there are twice as many, Ha Jun should be more than enough," Windshine said. "And so, my advice is this. The three of you should focus on defeating the ak-ma, and let Ha Jun handle the hollow men."

Yeong-Su considered Ha Jun. "One man against dozens. That may not be a good idea."

"But it may be our best strategy," Seong Min said. "We need to protect Su Won at all costs, as he is our best resource against the ak-ma." To Ha Jun, he asked, "Do you think you can fight off dozens of theses hollow men at once?"

Ha Jun glanced at Windshine. "I will do what I must to protect my older brothers and sister."

"Good," Seong Min said. "Then we should travel quickly so as not to give the ak-ma additional time to prepare for us." To Su Won, he asked, "The rancher said another group had come before us. Did you see them?"

Su Won shook his head. "If they made it to the fortress, they have been killed. There were only the hollow men there."

Seong Min looked in the direction they had come,

back towards the Hanguk Strait. On the other side was their home, Jeju. He remembered what he had told his wife before he left several days ago. Only by succeeding where others had failed could one distinguish themselves and become heroes.

"There would be no point in going," he said to the wide expanse behind them, "if everyone made it back alive."

CHAPTER TWELVE

They continued along the road until they reached a fork with a wooden sign that pointed right to Suncheon City. They continued straight to Jukdobong Forest, wanting to reach the fortress before the ak-ma could prepare further. They encountered no other travelers except for the ever-stinging mosquitoes and the clouds of gnats that hovered around them. The orchards had fallen away and replaced by fields. After they'd passed the fork to the city, they saw the tall trees of the forest looming ahead.

At the edge of Jukdobong, Seong Min took two tin pots from his pouch, lit the coals inside, and tied them to his waist. He filled the fire lance with powder and cut several fuses for quick access.

"I'll take the lead," Seong Min said, "and Yeong-Su and Su Won will follow. Older sister, please stay behind us, and Ha Jun will cover the rear."

Windshine conceded, and the five companions stepped into the forest. The tent caterpillar infestation had not spread past the orchards, and lush foliage topped the tall trees. The throaty drone of crickets, the sharp chirps of birds, and the rustling of leaves by small animals created a cacophony of natural songs. The companions tried to move quickly across the trail cutting through Jukdobong, but the heat beneath the trees drained the energy from their movements and slowed their trek to a crawl.

Eventually, they noticed a different sound pervading the birds and crickets. Seong Min gave a sign to pause, and the group stood still to listen to what sounded like dozens of branches snapping in two.

"What do you think it is?" Yeong-Su whispered.

As if in answer, the forest sprung to life. A cluster of six trees to Seong Min's left burst from the earth. Five of the trees were attached to the broad back of a dark brown beast. The sixth twisted itself until it was horizontal, and wide eyes opened above a gaping mouth of jagged fangs in its rough, bark-like face. The camouflaged creature supported itself on four muscular legs, and from its side, vine-shaped tendrils writhed. It reared back on its hind legs and bellowed a deep roar that shook the forest.

The running tree dashed at Seong Min.

Seong Min leapt to the side as the creature tore past him. He unshouldered his fire lance. The running tree slid to a stop, spun around, and roared at him again before it charged. With a steady hand, Seong Min lit the fuse at the end of the lance with the tin pot that dangled from his hip. He aimed it at the charging beat and took several steps back until the fuse hit the powder and ignited it. Flame leapt out of the dragon's mouth carved at the lance's opening and slammed into the oncoming beast. The creature roared with pain as its leaves curled in the fire.

Another cluster of trees rose up from the earth across from Yeong-Su, who unsheathed his sword to hack away at the tendrils that tried to wrap around his arms and legs. A third creature attacked Ha Jun, but his powerful sword strokes cut off one of its legs, and then another, before he stabbed the creature in its hardened chest and brought it down.

A fourth running tree went after Su Won, who grabbed the golden three-legged crow pendant in his hand. He chanted a string of interconnecting tones, and two spectral warriors materialized in front of him. They attacked the beast with cold swords that drove it back. Windshine saw a fifth beast rise from the ground behind Su Won, whose focus was on the two spectral warriors still engaged with the creature in front of him. Indecision made Windshine hesitate for a second before she called out, "Su Won, behind you!"

He spun to the running tree as it bore down upon him. One of the spectral warriors dematerialized from the creature it fought to materialize in front of Su Won. It lashed up with its cold blade and sliced through the creature's eye, a spray of sap splashing Su Won's clothes.

Su Won nodded a quick *thank you* to Windshine, but she was already casting a spell to scan the forest. More running trees came. They burrowed through the earth to reach the companions. If the brothers didn't leave now, they would be overwhelmed. Windshine sprinted through the melees waged around her to slip next to Seong Min.

"You must make it to the other side of the forest," she yelled at him. "There's too many of them, you'll never see them stalking you through the real trees."

Seong Min nodded as he poured more powder into his

lance. He looked over his shoulder to quickly access the situation before calling out, "Ha Jun, take the lead! Yeong-Su, Su Won, Windshine, follow him. I'm at the rear."

Ha Jun, surrounded by the limbs of the beasts that he had hacked off, leapt to Seong Min and charged the beast charging them. With a cry, he swept his sword upwards, and the creature fell as the blade cleaved its head in half. He pushed forward, followed by Su Won and his spectral warriors, Yeong-Su, and Windshine. Seong Min fought at the rear as the bursts of fire from his lance held the creatures at bay.

They made their way through the forest until the trees' attacks ended and a wide field opened up in front of them. They kept going to put distance between them and the Jukdobong Forest. When they saw that the running trees hadn't followed, they fell to the ground and gasped for air in the wet atmosphere. For many moments they couldn't stand as they struggled to breathe, their clothes drenched with sweat.

"We can't go back that way," Yeong-Su wheezed out.

Realization settled upon the companions that there would be no retreating. Before them rose the stone wall of Naganeupseong Fortress.

On the other side of the wall, the hollow men and the ak-ma waited.

CHAPTER THIRTEEN

The road leading from the forest to the wall ended at the fortress' metal gate. Yeong-Su suggested that they walk along the perimeter and go over the wall away from the entrance, but they had no rope, and no other means to scale the tall vertical surface. They had no choice but to approach the forbidding opening with weapons drawn.

When they reached the gate, Seong Min whispered, "There couldn't be a worse way to face our final enemy."

They studied the settlement beyond the entrance to see barracks and rectangular stone lodgings for soldiers. At the end of the long road stood the fortress, a wide, four-storied building with a high steeple roof and massive green double doors.

The companions stood at the threshold for several moments before stepping through the gate. A deep rumble of footsteps commenced in unison, echoing from the fortress in greeting of their entrance. The wide double doors swung open, and the hollow men marched out in columns, five across. Row after row of soldiers exited the building, their feet rising and falling at the same time, their arms swinging in the same rhythm, their short swords bouncing on their hips. The companions saw no place they could run as the army of hollow men marched down the fortress lane towards them, their green-eyed gazes empty yet unwavering upon the group of brothers.

"How many do you think there are?" Yeong-Su asked in awe, his face pale. "And from where did they all come?"

"The attacks on the farmhouses on the outskirts of the city," Su Won said. "The families like the one we saw that left nothing behind but spilled blood. These are them before us, cursed into these marionettes. There could be dozens. Maybe a hundred. Maybe more."

"Do you sense the ak-ma?" Seong Min asked Su Won.

He pointed at the fortress. "It lurks inside. We have to get there somehow, but there are so many hollow men standing in our way."

"Let Ha Jun deal with them," Windshine advised. "He must destroy the demon's forces. That will be the best way to draw it out."

Seong Min looked from Windshine to the marching columns of hollow men. The last row had finally cleared the fortress. He estimated at least two hundred made up the demon's army.

"It would be madness if anyone else suggested one boy take on this many soldiers." Seong Min looked at Ha Jun. "But we cannot go back, and those hollow men must be destroyed. Can you do this?"

Ha Jun turned to Windshine, and for a moment they stared into each other's eyes as the army continued its relentless march towards the companions.

"Ha Jun," she said, "that power inside of you. The one you keep buried deep down."

He averted his eyes to the ground.

"I know, it's something you're ashamed of. It feels too strong to be good, doesn't it?" She hesitated, and then reached out to lay a hand on his shoulder. He met her eyes again. "Too much power is often bad. But here, now, you have to release it, all of it, or you and your brothers will die.

"I'm sorry," she said to the group. "If Ha Jun cannot do this, you will never reach the ak-ma."

The reality of the situation sank in. They had come so far, and death waited for them.

Ha Jun released his sword from its sheath. "I will not allow my brothers to die."

He stepped away from the companions towards the oncoming soldiers. They wore no expression in their unnatural gray faces, and the steady blaze of their green eyes revealed no emotion. Whatever magic controlled them would show no mercy to his brothers and sister.

Ha Jun swallowed the dryness in his throat. For sixteen years, his father had trained him. He had spent his childhood enduring a regiment that no other could have borne. He had even learned to use the glyph sword when Windshine had specifically made it so humans would not be able to master the weapon. But was he ready? Was he good enough to prevail in this quest and become a hero?

Ha Jun didn't know, but at this moment, his doubts didn't matter. Seong Min, Yeong-Su, and Su Won would require his incredible strength. They needed his power, they needed him to give everything he could muster, then more. Ha Jun made a promise to himself that he would not allow even one of his older brothers to die.

He started at a steady walk towards the hollow men, and the walk became a jog. His muscular legs pumped faster beneath him, and the jog turned into a run. He kicked up dirt beneath his feet as he pushed himself harder, the ball of energy increasing in vibration, his heart thumping wilder as that awful power flooded his arms and legs. A cry built in his gut, spread into his chest, and erupted from Ha Jun's lips in a roar as he leapt high into the air. He sailed above the roofs of the barracks, his sword gripped tightly in both hands and held above his head. He soared higher than the steeple roof of the fortress. The air fluttered his clothes and whispered against his face. Ha Jun cleared row upon row of hollow men before he swung the blade in a downward arc and cried out in Elvish, *"Wind!"*

A massive gale swept down from the steel and slammed into the hollow men directly beneath him, crushing tens of them into the earth. He dropped through the air and landed on their corpses as the ground rumbled beneath his feet. Ha Jun sharpened the wind in his mind as he swung the sword in a low arc. He cried out again in Elvish, and the gale sliced through the abdomens of the nearest hollow men in a great circle, cutting a destructive swath through the puppet warriors.

Dozens of hollow men lay destroyed around him, their limbs ripped from their bodies or twisted at unnatural angles. The two wind inscriptions inscribed on the blade faded away. The hollow men drew their weapons as one, the release of their swords echoing through the barracks. Ha Jun stood in the midst of them, surrounded on all sides, his energy crackling inside of him. Many of the couple hundred hollow men remained, but they could only attack a few at a time without hacking away at one another. Ha Jun needed to be defensive of his blind spots and aggressive in his attacks.

The hollow men took a step towards him, their feet thudding on the ground like thunder. Ha Jun inhaled and waited.

The hollow men took another step towards him, and Ha Jun exhaled, long and low. The hollow men closest to him immediately lowered their swords, aiming the tips at his chest.

They rushed him as one, a circle of death closing in upon him. Ha Jun cocked his arm back and swung on his heel. His great blade clashed against their inferior ones, flinging their arms up and leaving them open for a second swipe. Without a pause, Ha Jun again cocked his arm back and spun, cutting through the hollow men's waists and severing them in half. They toppled where they stood. No blood spilled from their bodies, and no cries issued forth from their gray lips.

Others leapt into their place. The throng of hollow men bore down on him again, their expressions vacant. Their plan seemed only to tire him out with successive advancing waves.

Something latched onto Ha Jun's leg, and he looked down, surprised. One of the hollow men, whom he had crushed with his first attack, now grasped his ankle in a strong grip. The man filled out even as Ha Jun watched the limbs curling out like vines. The glowing green eyes stared emotionlessly at Ha Jun. With a cry, Ha Jun raised his sword to lop off the man's hand. The other hollow men rushed him at that exact moment. Ha Jun realized that he would have to use another of the inscriptions and cried out, *"Fire!"*

A tongue of flame engulfed the blade, and Ha Jun whipped it around in a circle. The fire swept from the blade in a cyclone of flame that set the charging hollow men alight. They fell back and slammed into those behind them. They, too, went up like dry kindling. For the first time, the hollow men retreated from Ha Jun en masse, and gave him space to avoid making contact with them.

Ha Jun raised his sword again to sever the arm that grabbed him and growled in pain as brambles suddenly grew from the hollow man's hand and speared his leg. Ha Jun brought down his sword in a swift strike to chop off the man's head. The grip didn't weaken, however, as the brambles impaled themselves further into his leg. Ha Jun crouched, then ripped the severed hand from his flesh. Blood sprayed the ground and flowed down his ankle.

The hollow men had recovered but gave Ha Jun a wide berth. Burnt corpses lay in black mounds around him. Ha Jun guessed that he had destroyed half, enough to significantly reduce their numbers. Fire was their weakness, but he only had one flame inscription left. The water and earth inscriptions would probably be useless, and electricity may not have the same effect on the wooden soldiers as fire had. He needed to be careful, since those who died could recover and attack him again unaware.

Ha Jun raised his sword and focused on the last fire inscription. If he could kill half of those remaining with this next strike, he could cut the last down with his sword arm. Ha Jun took a step towards them, and a stabbing pain laced through his leg again. He stumbled and scanned the ground for any hollow men who may have come back to life. He saw, instead, that the brambles had started to spread throughout his flesh, their pointed ends threading through his ankle and up his calf.

The hollow men took another step towards him as their footsteps echoed against the stonewalls surrounding the fortress, but now Ha Jun heard something else. He gritted his teeth as whispers filled his head. Voices, so many of them, hundreds all speaking in unison.

"Grow as one with us."

Ha Jun staggered under the weight of the command, the tumult of voices shrieking in his head, attempting to push out any other thought.

"We are branches of a powerful tree. We are old, and as part of a great whole, eternal. Grow as one with us."

The stabbing pain entered his side. Where the brambles had grown, his skin had turned gray. An urge to rip them from his body overtook him, but he sensed that would only cause more damage, would only drain the blood from his veins faster.

The hollow men charged him, and Ha Jun raised his sword high over his head in desperation.

"Be as one with us," the voices howled.

In response, Ha Jun cried out in Elvish, *"Earth!"*

He slammed his sword into the ground. The land beneath his feet fell away to crumble into a widening sinkhole. Ha Jun leapt out of the hole as the hollow men advanced and tumbled in. He landed on the outskirts of the rocky gulf and cried, *"Fire!"*

A blaze leapt from his blade again, and Ha Jun swept it across the sprawled hollow men. Fire leapt from the hole as the hollow men went up like torches. The shrill screams of South Hanguk men and women, and children, filled him. The horror of their pain froze his soul. He had to silence those anguished voices, and Ha Jun brought the sword down like a hammer's blow with a cry of, *"Earth!"*

The second earth inscription disappeared. The mountains surrounding the fortress shook at the power of his woe, and the hole opened further, crumbling hundreds of feet into the earth to take the burned hollow men deep into the ground. Ha Jun watched them tumble, but the brambles continued to thread through him.

Weakened, he fell to his knees, and his sword slipped from his fingers.

CHAPTER FOURTEEN

From a distance, the companions watched as Ha Jun collapsed.

"He needs us," Yeong-Su said, but Seong Min advised caution.

"The ak-ma still waits in the fortress. We don't know what else she has planned."

Yeong-Su nodded in agreement, but still urged haste. They made their way down the cracked and broken road, stepping over the area where Ha Jun had buried the hollow men. The marionette that had sprung back to life and grabbed Ha Jun's ankle in the midst of the battle had startled even them. They had forced themselves to hold back and wait to see if their youngest brother would need their help. Now they watched the overturned earth where the cursed families had sunk deep into the ground. Su Won prayed that their souls could find rest together in the afterlife. The strange magic that had animated the hollow men remained a mystery. None of the companions could be sure that they wouldn't resurrect at a moment's notice and crawl from the mud, their green eyes blazing in their emotionless gray faces.

Not wanting to take chances, the companions placed their feet with caution and probed the cracks with their weapons.

Once they reached Ha Jun, Yeong-Su gasped at the brambles crawling along Ha Jun's shivering body.

"Look!" He rushed to his younger brother to help him stand.

"No!" Su Won jumped in front of Yeong-Su and snatched his hand centimeters before he touched Ha Jun. The brambles, as if sensing uninfected flesh, unfurled from Ha Jun's skin towards the two companions.

"See how it reaches out? The unnatural growth is cursed," Su Won warned. "The hollow men are a plague. That's why entire families disappear. One of them gets infected, and the natural urge to help a brother, sister, a parent, spreads the infection to another. And then another. See!"

The brambles threaded their way through Ha Jun and sent spurts of blood to mists into the air and splatter on the ground. He opened his mouth to scream, and brambles erupted from his tongue and protruded out of his lips.

Yeong-Su spun to the monk. "We must do something! Quick, before he's killed!"

Su Won pushed Yeong-Su aside. "Don't forget, Little Brother," he said, "this is exactly why I was chosen for this quest."

He stepped towards Ha Jun and gripped the golden three-legged crow pendant around his neck. Chanting, he weaved a complicated sigil that left an impression that sizzled in the humid air. The temperature around them cooled, then became cold. A low tearing, as of reality splitting, drifted to their ears, and a spectral figure materialized from the sigil and floated towards Su Won. The figure wore a long hanbok that shimmered with a life of its own. Around his neck hung the same three-legged crow medallion as Su Won's.

"Ancient master." Su Won bowed to the specter. "I apologize for calling you from whatever busies you in the next realm. Our needs are great, and without the aid of our ancestors, we will be doomed to failure. If it is your will, help our younger brother suffering before us. If his time has not yet come, if there is more he is meant to do in this world of the living, stop his dying and save him from the plague consuming him alive."

The brambles continued to spread throughout Ha Jun. They crept across his face, the sharp points protruding from his chin right beneath his eye.

The long-dead monk turned from Su Won and floated towards Ha Jun. He paused and hovered near the stricken young man. His hanbok fluttered in some nether wind that didn't touch the living plane. He examined the curse that turned Ha Jun's skin a grayish color and gave the young man's eyes an unnatural green tint.

The specter lifted higher off the ground. A light surrounded him and intensified until the companions could barely keep their eyes open in its brilliance. The specter slammed into Ha Jun and came out the other side of the young man's body. Now the brambles covered the specter instead. They wrapped around him, tightening as if they would choke the life out of the dead. Their desperate attempts to strangle the monk proved useless, and the brambles withered and died within the freezing ether of the specter.

Ha Jun collapsed face first to the ground and lay there for several seconds, his breathing ragged and harsh.

Yeong-Su bounced from one foot to the other and glanced at Su Won, who forced him to wait a few moments before he nodded.

"It is safe now," he said with a gentle smile.

Yeong-Su rushed to Ha Jun's side and helped him to his feet.

"Younger Brother," Yeong-Su said, "you have shown great courage today. Truly are you a hero of South Hanguk!"

Seong Min also went to Ha Jun and clapped him on the back. "Your father will be proud."

At that, Ha Jun lifted his head and looked south towards Jeju and the long way they had traveled on the quest.

The specter approached Su Won, and the monk bowed again. The figure returned the bow, and faded back into the dissipating sigil.

"Ha Jun should be fine now," Su Won said in a tired voice. Weakness had stolen over the monk, and Seong Min went to his aid.

"But are you going to be fine, Brother?" he asked. Su Won nodded with a fatigued sigh.

"The spirits use me as a portal to this realm," he said. "Every time I summon them, they take a piece of my life energy. I've already brought them back from the other realm twice today. Once more, and I'll have to take a long rest to recuperate."

Seong Min bowed to him. "Thank you, Younger Brother, for your efforts."

Su Won began to return the bow, then froze. His eyes opened wide as terror crept over his face. The monk spun to the fortress, and a low moan slipped from his lips. He pointed beyond the doors inside of the steeple-roofed building.

"It's coming!" A harsh sob tore from his throat as uncontrollable shaking struck his stout body. "Evil. Ancient. Unforgiving." He backed away. "Coming!"

Seong Min followed Su Won's gaze to the fortress. His stare hardened. He glanced at Ha Jun and cursed. "Of course, now it would come, when we're in this terrible condition." He poured more powder into his fire lance. "This is the last of it," he said with another curse. "Yeong-Su, are you ready?"

Yeong-Su, who supported Ha Jun, said, "I will not let my companions die, so there is no choice. I will be ready."

Seong Min nodded and looked at his youngest brother next. "Ha Jun, you have fought well today, but our quest is not yet over. Can you offer us any more? Can you fight further?"

Ha Jun, leaning on Yeong-Su, wearily nodded. Bowing, he stepped away from his older brother and picked up his sword. "I will not fail my companions, so I too have no choice. I am ready. I will fight," he declared, but his words were weighed down with exhaustion and dropped from his mouth like stones.

Yeong-Su pointed towards the interior of the fortress with his sword. "Look. Something's coming out of the building."

At first, all they could make out was the shadowy

outlines of a figure. It walked slowly, boldly, and stepped casually out of the green double doors onto the path leading to the companions. It had velvet skin and wore a tunic of bright red with black swirls, and a round hat with a high golden point.

Windshine stumbled back in shock and gasped sharply. "Blythe?"

Her younger sister smiled brightly at her, her blue-brown eyes shining. "Windshine!"

A pause followed as all of the years they'd been separated expanded between them like a great gulf. Then the two sisters sprinted towards each other across this chasm of time, and amidst joyous laughter, they flung themselves into each other's arms in a powerful embrace.

"Blythe!" Windshine held her sister back to look at her, to inspect the details of her face, before pulling her closely to her chest again. "I can't believe it's you. Why are you here?"

Tears slipped from Blythe's blue-brown eyes as she hugged her sister. "Working," she admitted with an apologetic laugh. "Fate seems to have brought us together after so long. And it has been so very, very long, Older Sister. We have so much that we must discuss."

Blythe stepped away from Windshine, her smile so bright it imitated the sun. "I apologize, Sister, I have to take care of a couple of trivialities first."

Blythe turned to the four companions. She opened her arms wide, then swiftly closed them, her hands coming together in a thunderclap. A hail of needles exploded from her fingertips and slammed into Su Won. They tore through his body, his right arm sliced off, his legs obliterated, his stomach and chest ripped apart, his face skinned to the skull, his eyes speared to pop open and leak down the bones of his cheeks. The force of the blow lifted him up off of his feet and flung him back to land in a messy heap in the mud.

"No!" Seong Min screamed. Ha Jun turned to the monk in disbelief. Yeong-Su dashed to his fallen brother and dropped to his side, but they all knew that Su Won could not be alive after such an attack.

"Those monks are a real nuisance," Blythe said. "Of everything else about this land, I hate them the most." She spat with disgust. "The one who traveled with my group figured out that I was the one who made the hollow men before I had an opportunity to kill him."

Windshine stared open mouth at the shredded corpse that was Su Won. She slowly turned to her younger sister. "You made the hollow men?"

Blythe winked, then laughed and quickly hugged Windshine again. "I miss you so much, Older Sister. Four hundred years. Four centuries these humans kept us apart. Never again," she whispered. "We have so much work to do."

Windshine looked past Blythe at the fortress, then at the barracks, then at the three remaining companions. When Blythe separated from her again, she directed her gaze back onto her younger sister. "So much work?"

"Don't worry," Blythe said. "I've been laying down plans for decades."

A scream distracted them. Yeong-Su gazed at Blythe, the hatred in his eyes shining with a life of its own. His golden scale armor was splattered with the blood of his fallen companion, and he gripped his sword tightly in his hand. Again he screamed, and he charged Windshine's sister.

Blythe sighed in annoyance. "Like tiger mosquitoes buzzing in your ear."

Quickly she cast a spell and lazily waved her arm at Yeong-Su. A wall of fire spread from her fingers and struck him. Immediately, Yeong-Su's clothes and hair went up in flame. He howled in torment, his body an inferno in his golden scale armor. Seong Min and Ha Jun rushed to him, but the flame shot higher at their approach, the tongues licking out at them as Yeong-Su spun round and round, his shrill cries carrying across the barracks. Eventually, he collapsed, his limbs flailing as his screams became hoarse within the steadily burning fire.

"I hope the other two stay put," Blythe said. "I'll keep that one burning just a little longer," she nodded to Yeong-Su, who had stopped moving and now only roasted before his grief-stricken brothers, "to keep them occupied. I'd hate to kill them all. They'll be perfect in becoming new hollow men."

She turned to Windshine again. "I don't understand how they defeated my soldiers anyway," she said, puzzled. "Humans aren't the cleverest creatures."

Windshine stared at her sister as her mouth worked but no words were uttered.

"Windshine?" Blythe touched her on the arm and studied the confusion that raged across her sister's face. "You're really surprised to see me here, aren't you? I guess that makes sense. You thought these humans were coming here to kill an ak-ma?"

"Yes!" Windshine leaned closer to the individual before her. "You can't be my real sibling."

Blythe smiled. "Why? Do I not look like you remember? It has been a long time that the humans kept us apart, but I am your little sister. The same one Father put in your care on the ship that sailed us across the seas. The same one who stepped with you, hand in hand, on this land of South Hanguk, and was taken from you by the Emperor of this country."

Windshine pointed to broken Su Won and burning Yeong-Su. "But you're killing humans!"

"Of course," Blythe said. "This is just the beginning of the plan."

"The plan!" Windshine snapped. "You keep mentioning a plan, but I have no idea what you mean by it. What plan do you speak of?"

An impish smile played on Blythe's lips. "Do you remember what the wisest of elves realized in our home country? The only way to truly end conflict?" The smile spread further. "I've thought of nothing else for centuries. Complete elimination of the enemy. The genocide of the people of South Hanguk, Windshine. I'm going to kill them all."

CHAPTER FIFTEEN

Was this really her sister? Was Blythe declaring war upon the human race?

Windshine reached out into the world around her. She opened her senses to the possibility of deception. The barracks and building, both were real stone and wood; the ground she stood upon, the road leading through the fortress, wasn't an illusion. She probed the figure standing before her who smiled that casual smile of murderous intent, and she sensed that it truly was a Dark Elf.

To the right of the sisters, Seong Min leapt up from Yeong-Su and bellowed in rage. He lit the fuse of his fire lance and charged Blythe.

She sighed with frustration. "Maybe they aren't the perfect hosts to become hollow men." She lifted her arm. "Families are more docile. Infect the children, the mother falls while the father quickly follows. Perhaps that's the best way to build a new army."

She began to wave her hand in Seong Min's direction, but Windshine caught her wrist. Seong Min reached them and aimed the fire lance at Blythe as the fuse hit the powder with an explosion of flame. Blythe twisted from Windshine's grasp and uttered a quick spell that pushed her older sister out of the path of the attack. Both elves spun across the dusty road.

Blythe raised her hand again towards Seong Min. Windshine broke her momentum, dug her booted heels into the ground, and pounced forward to stand between her sister and her target.

Blythe aborted her attack and gave Windshine a confused look. "You're in my way. You needn't be worried; I can always find more humans to make hollow men. These quest males are annoying, anyway. Not as good at submitting as women and children."

"Blythe!" Windshine tried to comprehend what was going on. Had she fallen asleep and entered a nightmare? She probed reality once again but had to accept that this wasn't a dream. She was awake and stood in front of her younger sister who was steadfast in her decision to kill the company of young men that Windshine had travelled with from Jeju.

"Blythe!" Windshine's mouth opened, closed, and opened again. "You can't kill the people of South Hanguk!"

"Why?"

Windshine sputtered at the absurdity of the question. "What do you mean, why? You can't annihilate an entire country of people. Father sent us here because the other Dark Elves decided that that was the answer to their age-old conflict. But he knew it wasn't. Genocide is not the way to resolve conflict."

Blythe scoffed. "Don't parrot Father's last words,

Windshine. He was wrong. Total elimination of the enemy is the only way to bring about peace." She kept her hand raised, magic sparkling at her fingertips. "In any country, only one mode of thinking must reign supreme. What doesn't work, what can't exist, is a dozen, or hundreds of opinions. This is what our home country was, splintered factions at each other's throats. But there is no peace in variety. We've already witnessed that! Differences lead to arguments. Arguments lead to conflicts. Conflicts lead to war. Year after year, generation after generation. A foolish, stupid waste of time. No one wants to admit it in the beginning, but everyone knows it's the truth. One side must win, and all others must be obliterated."

"Blythe!" Windshine gaped at her sister. "These words, the evil in them. You can't really think this way."

The brown in Blythe's blue eyes became agitated, like sand kicking up into a dust storm. "You claim what I want is evil?" A red hue touched the magic at her fingertips. "Was it not evil for humans to separate us? To keep women with women, and men with men, so that we could not love? So that we could not bear children? They put us two in a province, and even then, they keep us separated so that we can't even speak in our own language."

The magic at her fingertips blazed a deep, fiery red.

"Even now I'm speaking Hangugeo to you! It's been so long since I used my own language, and instinctively I speak this foreign drivel to you, my own sister!"

The magic blazed around her hand. The brown of her pupils swirled in violent vortices within the blue of her corneas.

"Do you think if we went to their governors," Blythe said, switching to Elvish, "to their Emperor, and implored them to change the laws, that they would listen? Four hundred years ago they mandated that we be separated. For us, it's a painful memory. For them, it's established culture. A way of life they were born knowing, for generations. You think that's going to change if we just ask for it? They've had distrust of Dark Elves bred into them, and nothing is going to reverse that!"

Windshine grimaced at how difficult she found it to understand her younger sister's Elvish. Blythe had come here when she was barely two hundred years old, still considered a child to Dark Elves, safely protected at home and largely ignorant of their country at large. She'd lived now among the people of South Hanguk twice as long as she'd been alive and had barely spoken the Elvish language for centuries. A Hangugeo accent had infected the rhythm of her speech, and Windshine struggled to comprehend all that her sister said.

"Blythe." This conversation exhausted her. "Blythe, you're right." She looked around at the Naganeupseong Fortress. "What the humans did to us was wrong. But try to see it from their perspective. Strange people land on their shores. When we first arrived, we thought nothing of demonstrating some of our magic. Small spells to us, but overwhelming from their point of view. We didn't realize we were terrifying them until it was too late. They feared we would wage war upon them, so they did what they thought was necessary. They let us live here, but they did it in a way that they believed would weaken us and keep us under their control."

"They were wrong! We could have always conquered them. Even twenty-five of us were enough."

This was true. The Dark Elves had always possessed

the ability to conquer the people of South Hanguk, but they had come here from a war-torn country with dreams of peace. No one wanted to start another war in these lands. But what if the Emperor had allowed them to remain together? What if they had been able to love, to have families, to become a part of this country instead of being isolated from it and each other? If the humans had allowed them to integrate, to find happiness in simply being alive, perhaps Blythe wouldn't have developed the ideas she had. Perhaps there wouldn't be so much hatred in her magic. But then, that was always the Dark Elves' weakness. Hatred was the basis for their greatest spells and weapons.

"Now all of the people of South Hanguk will die by our hands," Blythe said, "and we'll start a new kingdom here, in this country. And it'll be populated only by elves."

"No, Blythe." Tears filled Windshine's eyes. "For all the wrongs the humans have visited upon us, I will not be party to genocide. And I will not allow you to kill off an entire country of people. I've lived a thousand years, and still I have not found a lasting solution to conflict. But something deep inside of me knows that, though genocide may be an answer, it is the worst one to choose. Life in all its diversity, as difficult as it is, it's also essential."

Blythe returned her sister's gaze, their blue brown eyes locked onto each other. "What will you do, then?"

"What I must, to end this nightmare and wake up."

CHAPTER SIXTEEN

Even though she was younger, Blythe had always been considered a genius at spell casting. In order to stop her little sister, Windshine needed to be careful so as not to cause her too much harm.

"Binding." Windshine's blue tunic shivered at the command. Wrappings unraveled from the fabric and snaked towards Blythe. Her sister danced away from them, evading the tendrils as she chanted. A buzzing light appeared around her hands, and she sliced through the cloth as it attempted to entangle her. She hopped onto the thatch roof of the soldier lodgings.

"Windshine." She shook her head. "Why are you doing this?"

"Fly." Windshine's boots lifted her off the ground to soar over the barracks. "Come to the Emperor with me. Talk to him and take the punishment for your crimes."

Blythe narrowed her eyes. "I've killed hundreds of humans already. He won't forgive me for that, and nor should he. Once blood is spilled, it'll keep being spilled until one side or the other is extinguished. Only a fool believes otherwise."

Blythe waved her hand. A gale swept towards Windshine and slammed into her. She flipped in the strong winds, breath stolen from her as the ground became the sky and the sky became the ground. She saw her sister send another wall of wind her way, and Windshine uttered, "Shield."

A vibrating bubble erupted from her tunic to form around her as the gale smashed against the barrier. She immediately realized that even if the spell had hit her, it wouldn't have done more than knock her to the ground. Blythe didn't hate her, so her magic lacked the true potency of the Dark Elves. Yet her little sister did have a point about the Emperor. He would never forgive her. Blythe hadn't just killed companions on a quest. She had killed women and children, fathers protecting their families. She had used their love against each other, the plague of the brambles infecting all those that touched it as they sought to comfort the infected. The people of South Hanguk would want her to pay the ultimate price for her betrayal.

Below Windshine, Seong Min withdrew a dagger that had been tucked into his hanbok. He rushed Blythe. Her sister's face twisted with anger. She cupped her hand, and a spear of bright red light materialized in her palm. Seong Min raised the dagger to throw at Blythe, but she was faster and hurled the glowing spear at him. Windshine touched her hat and said, "Wall."

The stone lodging beneath Blythe's feet ripped apart and sped ahead of the spear. They reconstructed before the spear could strike Seong Min, and the hastily constructed wall exploded at the impact, blasting Seong Min back.

Blythe hovered above the destroyed lodgings and turned to Windshine. Their gazes met. "I cannot kill you, sister," Blythe said. "But I can entrap you until you've thought this through. You'll come to see my way is the only path forward for the Dark Elves in this country."

"You'll never convince me that the murder of an entire people is the right solution."

Her sister spread her arms, and the moisture in the air pulled into vortexes above her upturned palms. They spun faster until they were two massive tornadoes, the winds from them howling with amazing force. Windshine raised her arms in front of her eyes to block the screaming air. Blythe flung the tornado in the right palm, and it tore across the ground towards Windshine.

"Shield!"

The cyclone struck Windshine and whirled around her creating a prison of wind. Blythe slowly closed her hand, and the tornado constricted, the shield's force buckling beneath the incredible pressure of the swirling gales. Windshine held many destructive words woven into the fabric of her clothes, but she would not use them against her sister. She must figure out a way to incapacitate Blythe by using the least amount of deadly force.

Seong Min stood from the rubble. Blood dripped from scratches along his face and arms, and his hanbok lay torn open across his chest. He searched for the dagger he had dropped, found it, and turned to Blythe again. She noticed him try to approach her, unseen. The tornado in her right hand took on a bright red hue. She flicked the cyclone from her palm, and it raced towards him, ripping up the ground and sending chunks of earth flying with its passage.

Seong Min bellowed in defiance as the tornado roared at him, his dagger raised before him. Right before it struck, Ha Jun dropped from the air next to him, snatched his older brother in his arms, and leapt out of the path of destruction. He sailed over the barracks and landed in front of the green doors of the fortress, where he settled Seong Min safely on his feet.

Blythe gazed at Ha Jun, who took a step towards her, his sword in his hand. The energy inside of him flared in intensity, filling him with a crimson aura. Blythe backed away from him, and Ha Jun took another step towards her, his face twisting into a snarl. She raised her arm to cast another spell, but her hand quivered. The water in the air froze into an ice ball, then shattered into dozens of jagged shards, their sharp points glistening. She darted behind them and inhaled. Her breath exhaled from her lips in a powerful explosion that hurtled the ice shards at Ha Jun with tremendous speeds.

"Water!" Ha Jun cried in Elvish and swept the sword in a downward arch. A wave swept from the blade, catching the shards up in the torrent that then swept towards Blythe. She tried to evade it, but a massive crest rose up and crashed down, swallowing her amidst its eddies.

"Blythe!" The cyclone of air still threatened to crush Windshine, and she said, "Extension."

The tunic filled the bubble, and it expanded out dispersing the wind into the buildings around her, which were ripped from the ground and tossed around the fortress. Windshine flew over the water that flooded the fortress and spied Blythe clinging to one of the still standing lodgings. Blythe pulled herself from a current attempting to suck her under and managed to balance on the stonewall of the building. She gazed in awe at Ha Jun, fear sweeping the velvet features of her face.

"So much rage," she breathed out. "So much hatred."

Blythe pointed to the sky, and the clouds darkened. Thunder rumbled through the canyons, the ground shaking with the deep, resounding echoes. Lightning strikes flashed above the surrounding mountains, and sudden explosions blew trees apart. Blythe opened her hand. Five bolts struck her fingers. They collected in a crackling ball of vibrating electricity. She closed her fingers around the lighting in her palm and flung it at Ha Jun.

The sixteen-year-old did not flinch. He roared in rage, cocked his sword back, and swung. The Elvish blade contacted the ball of lightning and it ricocheted back at Blythe. She dropped her shoulder to the side, and the ball sped past her back into the clouds. Ha Jun didn't hesitate, crouched, and leapt at Blythe. He hurled the sword at her. It spun in the air, the blade blazing with electricity as it impaled her chest. Bright light flared, and a powerful current raced through Blythe. Her head burst into flame as her tunic melted against her flesh. The sword slammed into the wall surrounding the fortress, the blade lodging into the stone.

"Blythe!" Windshine soared down to land beside her. She dropped to her knees as sobs tore through her. Blythe's body convulsed, her blackened lips pulled back from her teeth, her mouth opened wide in a scream. No sound issued forth, for death had already claimed her.

CHAPTER SEVENTEEN

Time lost meaning. Moments could have been days could have been years. Windshine gazed at the shriveled husk that had been her sister and marveled at the absurdity of Elvish power. She could create weapons to kill thousands, but she could do nothing to bring her little sister back from the dead.

Footsteps approached, and she turned slightly as Ha Jun came to stand beside her. What were the appropriate words for the killer of your sister to say? At a moment like this, there weren't many utterances that would make sense, but Ha Jun found the perfect words in the form of a question.

"Do you hate me now?"

"It would be easy to hate you," she said, her voice tight with emotion. "It's always easier to hate. There are usually so many better reasons to, and not nearly as many reasons to let go and forgive."

Tears slid down Windshine's cheeks. "Father sent us from our homeland so that we wouldn't learn the ways of vengeance. It's an infection, spreading from person to person and generation to generation. Before you know it, you're fighting a forever war."

Ha Jun hesitated, then laid a hand on Windshine's shoulder. "Before you stopped speaking Hangugeo, I heard what your sister said. I don't blame her for wanting to kill humans. I never realized everything that had happened to the elves in the ancient history of South Hanguk. I'm sorry humans treated you the way we did."

Windshine nodded. "So am I."

Silence again, until Ha Jun asked, "What do we do now? The quest is over."

Windshine sighed and pushed herself to her feet. Ha Jun's hand fell from her shoulder. "The sword is yours, and all of its power."

With all of the knowledge gleaned from ten centuries, she studied the face of this sixteen-year-old human. Lines of fatigue spread from the corners of his eyes. The youthful exuberance she had seen in his features days before had been melted away by exhaustion and death.

"You can become a great man one day," she told him. "A governor of a province, or even of higher status in the Emperor's court. With that weapon, your possibilities are limitless."

"And so are my responsibilities," Ha Jun said. In that moment, the face of the boy became the face of a man. *Perhaps*, Windshine thought, *the sword that killed my sister is in as good of hands as it could be in this human land.*

"And you," Ha Jun said. "What will you do?"

Windshine looked upon Blythe for a final time. "I am the recorder of the adventures of heroes because I will be here long after all of you are gone. But I must ask you and

Seong Min for permission to lie. I shall say you slew an ak-ma at the end of your journey, and not a Dark Elf. If the truth got out, it might start a war. Humans won't want that. My people are exceptionally skilled at violence."

Windshine walked past Ha Jun towards Seong Min still at the fortress doors. "Take your sword, Little Brother, and bury my sister. It's time we returned to Jeju."

The End

ABOUT TODD SULLIVAN

Todd Sullivan teaches English as a Second Language, and English Literature & Writing in Asia. He has had numerous short stories, novelettes, and novellas published across several countries, including Thailand, the U.K., Australia, the U.S., and Canada. He is a practitioner of the sword-fighting martial arts, kumdo/kendo, and has trained in fencing (foil), Muay Thai, Capoeira, Wing Chun, and JKD. He graduated from Queens College with a Master of Fine Arts in Creative Writing and received a Bachelor of Arts in English from Georgia State University. He attended the Bread Loaf Writers' Conference and the National Book Foundation Summer Writing Camps. He currently lives in Taipei, Taiwan, and looks forward to studying Mandarin.

Printed in Great Britain
by Amazon

17899253R00079